"Take off yo[ur clothes," he demanded, locking his office door.

Sunny laughed. "Don't be shy, now, Kirk. I know how difficult it is for you to say what's on your mind."

He stalked to the well-worn institutional-style sofa. He started heaving piles of books and file folders off it and flinging them to the floor. "It's been eighteen days since we made love, *really* made love—"

"But who's counting, right?" she teased.

"—and I'm more than willing to strip you myself, but if I try it, in my present enthusiastic frame of mind, I might just end up ripping that uniform to shreds." He grinned. "How will you explain that to your boss?"

She plucked at the ugly pink fabric. "Polyester, remember? Not so easy to tear."

He swept the last papers from the sofa and turned back to her, his expression more heated than she'd ever seen it. "Try me."

Dear Reader,

When four romantically minded high school girls vow to find each other husbands if any of them are still single at age thirty, they have no idea how complicated it will make their lives twelve years later! I'm giving each of our matchmaking pals—Raven, Charli, Sunny and Amanda—her own story, one each month, in THE WEDDING RING Harlequin Temptation miniseries.

One Eager Bride To Go reunites high school sweethearts Sunny and Kirk. It's as if they haven't been separated for the past dozen years—until a devastating secret threatens their happiness.

The Wedding Ring matchmaking pact was set into motion in December 2000 with *Love's Funny That Way,* when Raven Muldoon fell in love with the brother of the man her pals had chosen as her future husband. Last month Charli entered into a marriage of convenience that became decidedly inconvenient when she fell in love with her husband in *I Do, But Here's the Catch.* Finally, in March, two-time divorcée Amanda, determined to remain single, will try to outwit her matchmaking friends with a phony fiancé in *Fiancé for Hire.*

I hope you'll join me for all four of these fun, sexy WEDDING RING stories. You can visit me on the Web at www.pamelaburford.com, or write to me (include an SASE) at P.O. Box 1321, North Baldwin, NY 11510-0721.

Love,

Pamela Burford

ONE EAGER BRIDE TO GO
Pamela Burford

ONE EAGER BRIDE TO GO

Copyright © 2001 by Pamela Burford Loeser.

All rights reserved. Except for use in any review, the reproduction or utilization of this work in whole or in part in any form by any electronic, mechanical or other means, now known or hereafter invented, including xerography, photocopying and recording, or in any information storage or retrieval system, is forbidden without the written permission of the publisher, Harlequin Enterprises Limited, 225 Duncan Mill Road, Don Mills, Ontario, Canada M3B 3K9.

All characters in this book have no existence outside the imagination of the author and have no relation whatsoever to anyone bearing the same name or names. They are not even distantly inspired by any individual known or unknown to the author, and all incidents are pure invention.

This edition published by arrangement with Harlequin Books S.A.

® and TM are trademarks of the publisher. Trademarks indicated with ® are registered in the United States Patent and Trademark Office, the Canadian Trade Marks Office and in other countries.

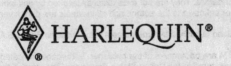

HARLEQUIN®

TORONTO • NEW YORK • LONDON
AMSTERDAM • PARIS • SYDNEY • HAMBURG
STOCKHOLM • ATHENS • TOKYO • MILAN • MADRID
PRAGUE • WARSAW • BUDAPEST • AUCKLAND

To my son, Daniel Loeser,
who always makes me proud.

ISBN 0-373-25920-4

ONE EAGER BRIDE TO GO

1

"OH NO YOU DON'T! Not him. No way!" Sunny Bleecker gaped at the man striding through the ballroom's open pocket doors some thirty feet away. His height made him easy to spot over the heads of the wedding guests milling around.

Automatically Sunny tried to back away, but her friends Raven Radley and Amanda Coppersmith, standing on either side of her, kept a firm grip on her arms. Sunny's fingers tightened painfully on the bridal bouquet she'd just caught.

"Hear us out," Raven said.

"You must be nuts!" Sunny cried. "You were supposed to find me a husband—as in a *brand-new* guy, someone I've never laid eyes on before. Not—not..." With her arms imprisoned, she nodded helplessly at the latecomer to Charli and Grant's wedding reception, this specter from her past, now scanning faces as he wove his way through the throng of guests.

He'd let his hair grow, she noticed, that pale wheat-colored hair that looked as thick and soft now as it had been when the two of them graduated from high school. Then, he'd worn it short, practically a crew cut. Now it fell almost to his shoulders.

Charli detached herself from her bridegroom, Grant Sterling, to lay a reassuring hand on Sunny's shoulder. Charli looked so lovely in her white satin wedding gown, her long, dark hair pulled back in a chignon encircled with cream rosebuds. Of the four best friends, the four lifelong pals who comprised the Wedding Ring matchmaking club, Carlotta "Charli" Rossi was the one who'd never expected to get married. Yet here she was, with her sexy, devoted husband, the two of them deliriously in love—the latest Wedding Ring success story.

Charli and Grant had exchanged vows during a beautiful, moving church wedding followed by this sumptuous reception for 320 guests. Three months earlier Raven Muldoon had married Hunter Radley, and they'd just announced they were expecting a baby.

Two down, two to go. Sunny had just turned thirty, so it was now officially time for the other three members of the Wedding Ring, her best friends in the world, to find her a husband. That was the solemn pact they'd made twelve years earlier at the end of high school, and it was an obligation they all took seriously.

For Raven and Charli, the pact had worked. And Sunny suspected that even Amanda, who resisted the idea of walking down the aisle again after two failed marriages, would change her mind when her turn came in a few months.

But it was supposed to be Sunny's turn now, and look who the Wedding Ring had chosen for her!

A few moments earlier, Sunny's friends had wished her a happy thirtieth birthday. "What do you want more than anything?" Raven had asked her. "What have you *always* wanted more than anything?"

That was a no-brainer. A husband. A husband and children. It was all Sunny had ever wanted, for as long as she could remember. The kind of loving happiness her parents had known for thirty-three years.

Then Charli had announced that the Wedding Ring had made its decision; they'd chosen a prospective husband for Sunny. Raven had reminded her that under the terms of their pact, she was required to date the chosen man for a full three months, as long as he was interested.

"I know the rules," Sunny had muttered. "Now, show me my man!"

That was when they'd pointed out Kirk Larsen, just entering the ballroom.

"You guys cheated!" Sunny struggled without success to yank her arms from her friends' unyielding grasp. "I was supposed to get a *new* man! Made from all-new materials—none of this recycled stuff. What are you trying to pull?"

Hunter spoke up. "Sunny, I don't think they're trying to pull anything. As I understand it, you and Kirk were pretty tight back in high school."

"*Were!*" Sunny responded. "Note the past tense.

Kirk went away to college—to California, no less, clear across the country!—and left me behind. If I wasn't good enough for him then—"

"Come on, Sunny, it wasn't like that." Raven's expression was chiding, but her voice was gentle.

"How do *you* know what it was like?" Sunny's face stung with angry heat. "It happened to *me*, not *you*!"

Grant rubbed his chin. "Maybe this wasn't such a good idea."

Amanda's frustration was evident. "Listen, Sunny. You two *were* tight back then, you really cared about each other, and face it. You haven't felt the same way about a guy since." She softened her tone, as well as her grip on Sunny's arm. "Charli and Raven and I just want you to be happy. We knocked heads trying to come up with the right guy for you, and then when Kirk's mom told my mom he was back in town, well..." She looked at her friends for support. "The pieces just kind of fell into place."

"You two have very similar personalities," Raven said persuasively. "You're both lighthearted. Buoyant. You're made for each other."

"Give him a chance," Charli said.

"Three months." Amanda held up three fingers. "That's all we're asking."

Sunny had been tracking Kirk's progress across the ballroom. He moved with a long-legged, masculine grace that she still recognized after all these years. He hadn't noticed her yet. "This is all probably for nothing," she said in a small voice. "I mean he—he probably won't be interested."

"Well, if he is..." Charli said.

Sunny sighed. If he was interested, she was obligated to give the relationship three months. She'd spent a dozen years trying to get over her teenage heartbreak, and not until she set eyes on Kirk Larsen again did she realize she hadn't done a very good job of it. "Does he...does he know he and I are supposed to...?"

Amanda made a face. "I thought you said you knew the rules. Rule number two—the man must not be told he's part of a matchmaking scheme."

"Until after he's been reeled in and landed," Hunter added, with a mischievous grin.

"You have no right to complain," Amanda told him. "You're not even the one who was *supposed* to be reeled in and landed. We'd targeted your brother for that honor."

Raven released Sunny to cuddle up to Hunter, the *brother* of the man the Wedding Ring had chosen for her. "Well, I for one am glad your first choice didn't work out."

"Which only shows," Sunny said, "that the Wedding Ring isn't infallible. We made the wrong choice for Raven, and maybe you guys have made the wrong choice for me."

"Shh!" Charli hissed, cocking her head toward their quarry, who was fast approaching.

Kirk's gaze was fixed exclusively on the bride. He

appeared not to notice Sunny or any of his other old pals. "Charli!" He gave her a bear hug and a kiss on the cheek, before holding her at arm's length. His pale blue eyes crinkled at the corners. "You are without a doubt the most beautiful bride I've ever seen."

Charli blushed furiously. It was no secret that she'd always considered herself plain and mousy. Only when she'd fallen in love with Grant had her singular beauty come to the fore. Sunny knew that Charli's newfound self-assurance had much to do with it.

Sunny's heart pounded in giddy anticipation as Charli introduced Kirk to her bridegroom. Kirk congratulated Grant and apologized for his late arrival. "My son has an ear infection. My folks are babysitting, but I wanted to wait till his fever went down before I left him."

Sunny's frantic heartbeat stuttered. A dizzying wash of heat swept her. He was married. So much for the Wedding Ring. So much for rekindling the old flame. Even if she wanted to. Which she didn't.

Sunny didn't dare look at Amanda or Raven. She couldn't bear to see the dismay on their faces, to feel their chagrin as they realized their plan had fizzled before it ever got off the ground. She took a step back, and another one, trying to blend into the teeming crowd of wedding guests.

Kirk and Amanda exchanged hugs, then he greeted Raven, who introduced him to Hunter. Raven glanced around, spotted Sunny trying to shuffle out of sight, and hauled her back by the arm. "Look who else is here," Raven said.

Kirk's electric-blue gaze lit on Sunny, snatching her breath and making her light-headed. He blinked, slowly, and his mouth curved in a tender smile. "Sunny."

His hand settled on her shoulder as he leaned in for a kiss—on the cheek, Sunny assumed, until his lips touched hers, lightly, fleetingly.

Well, that made sense, she supposed. This was, after all, the man she'd lost her virginity to, all those years ago. Her first serious boyfriend.

Okay, her *only* serious boyfriend. She could understand why her friends had latched on to the idea of reuniting them. What Amanda had said was true. Sunny hadn't felt the same way about any other man since Kirk had boarded his flight for California twelve years earlier.

So where was Mrs. Kirk Larsen today? Back in the Golden State, no doubt, keeping the home fires burning while her husband and son made this pilgrimage to Kirk's boyhood home on Long Island.

Say something, she commanded herself.

"Kirk." Sunny pasted on a polite smile. "It's been...a long time."

Something passed behind his eyes, something akin to sadness, and then it was gone. Sunny wondered if she'd imagined it. After all, she hadn't seen Kirk in over a decade; she couldn't expect to read his moods as easily as she once had.

His face had matured. No traces of boyhood soft-ness remained. Likewise, his body had lost its youth-ful whip-leanness. Though he was obviously still fit and trim, his oatmeal-colored suit jacket could not conceal broad shoulders and a sinewy thickness in all the right places.

Sunny became aware of an awkward watchfulness on the part of her friends. She felt more than foolish after that contentious discussion right before Kirk joined them. *The man's spoken for, okay?* she was tempted to tell them. *So just relax already!*

The emcee announced, "It's time for the garter cer-emony. Grant, bring your beautiful bride up here!"

The guests gathered on the sidelines as Grant led Charli onto the dance floor and settled her on the chair that had been placed there. Shyly she dragged the hem of her gown to just above her knee. A frilly blue garter came into view, eliciting an enthusiastic response from the male guests and a few strains of stripper music from the band. Grant lingered over the chore of sliding the garter down her leg, taking his time, whispering something that had his bride coloring up and laughing behind her hand.

The emcee wasted no time calling up all the un-married men to try to catch the garter. Sunny was looking forward to this. A few minutes earlier, Charli had tossed her bouquet and Sunny had prac-tically tackled all the other single women to secure possession of it. That meant she was destined to be-come the next bride. It might be meaningless tradition, but hey, you never knew. Tradition also dictated that the man who caught the bride's garter would be the next fellow to tie the knot.

As the single men congregated some distance behind him, Grant prepared to toss the garter over his shoulder. Hunter nudged Kirk. "You heard the man—get out there."

Was Hunter clueless or what? Sunny wondered. They'd all heard Kirk mention his son.

Kirk slid his hands into his pockets. "That's okay, I'll just watch."

Laughing, Hunter gave him a hard shove, propelling him toward the action. "It doesn't work that way. You've got a garter to catch!"

Kirk gave in, with obvious apathy, standing at the rear of the group with his hands still crammed in his pockets. The drumroll began.

Sunny turned to Hunter and asked, "Why did you do that? Isn't Kirk—"

Hunter cupped his hands around his mouth to shout, "Long bomb, Grant! Hit the back wall!"

Balling up the garter, Grant threw it with vigor, sending it sailing high over the heads of the men waiting to catch it. Sunny watched the scrap of blue lace arc directly toward Kirk as the other guys tripped over their feet and slammed into one another in an effort to snag it. At the last second, a bemused-looking Kirk simply reached up and plucked the thing out of midair.

Hunter let out a whoop of triumph. Sunny tried to

question him again about Kirk's marital status, but she never got the chance as Raven and Amanda turned her bodily and marched her onto the dance floor toward the chair Charli had vacated.

Sunny's heart stumbled. "Wait a minute. Time out."

She knew the drill; she'd witnessed it often enough. The guy who caught the garter then had to put it on the gal who caught the bouquet.

She refused to sit. "Listen, I don't think this is such a good—"

Her friends shoved her onto the chair, hard, as the emcee ordered Kirk front and center. Then it was just the two of them, in the middle of the huge dance floor, ringed by hundreds of cheering, clapping wedding guests.

The emcee was giving Kirk instructions, suggestive little pearls of wisdom. Sunny sat clutching the bouquet in her sweaty fingers, her trembling knees clamped together beneath her ankle-length, vintage chiffon dress.

She looked up at Kirk, now standing before her with the silly lace garter dangling from his long, suntanned fingers. She made herself meet his eyes, expecting to see, at best, mild annoyance. Instead he wore the strangest expression, half melancholic, half amused.

Kirk knelt on one knee before her, like a man preparing to ask for his lady's hand in marriage. A wave of scalding heat crawled up Sunny's face.

"I'm sorry about this," she said in an undertone, for his ears only, wondering where the urge to apologize had come from. But she knew where. She glanced at her Wedding Ring pals and their husbands, standing at the edge of the crowd, shouting encouragement.

"You are?" he asked, a funny smile lighting his blue, blue eyes. He grasped the fluttery hem of her dress, multiple layers of floral chiffon in muted pastel tones.

Good Lord, he'd turned into a beautiful man—so handsome it almost hurt to look at him. Sunny's knees locked even tighter together. Her fingers cramped around the wrapped stem of the bouquet. "What I mean is...there's a little too much history between us. This is—" She jumped as he inched the hem up her calves. A breathy chuckle escaped her. "Well, it's weird, that's all."

"You let your hair grow." Slowly, very slowly, Kirk raised the hem of her dress, his eyes never straying from hers.

Sunny reached up to finger the long, wavy, auburn strands draped over her breast. She'd twisted the side pieces into loose, reddish brown ropes and secured them behind her head with an antique marcasite barrette. Back in high school her hair had been a short, curly cap.

He added, "You look like one of those ethereal beauties in a Pre-Raphaelite painting."

The compliment suffused Sunny with a warm

glow, although her ignorance embarrassed her. She didn't know a Pre-Raphaelite painting from a Cubist. That wasn't the sort of knowledge one gained waiting tables at the local diner.

"You grew your hair, too," she observed. "It looks nice." *Does your son's mother like it?*

Her hem had risen as far as her knees. Kirk said, "If you don't unlock your legs, I might have a bit of trouble getting this thing on you." He glanced at the boisterous crowd, spurring on the action with applause and choice bits of advice. "Just how much of a show do you want to give these folks?"

Sunny swallowed hard. She took a slow, deep breath and willed her tense legs muscles to relax. Delicately she nudged one foot forward.

"No shoes," he observed, with a small smile. "Still the wild child, I see."

"I took them off to give me a better chance of catching the bouquet."

"Tough competition?"

Sunny grinned, recalling how she'd nearly lost out to one of Charli's cousins from Detroit, the tall one with the troweled-on makeup and the hot pink tube dress. "Yeah, but I'm tougher."

"That's one word I'd never have used to describe you. *Tough*." Kirk pulled the layers of chiffon higher still, letting the hem settle partway up her thighs, as the rowdier male guests hooted in approval. He lifted her foot and rested it on the leg he knelt on. His thigh felt hard and muscular under the sole of her foot, and hot, even through his dress slacks and her nylon stockings.

He slipped the frilly garter over her toes, up her ankle and calf, to the accompaniment of wolf whistles and more suggestive music. He slid it over her knee and higher. Sunny had to work hard to keep her breathing even. As he positioned the garter a decorous two inches above her knee, the tips of his fingers happened to brush just under the hem of her dress.

Kirk went still. He locked his gaze with hers while his warm fingertips, hidden from view, traced the top edge of her stocking and the clasp connecting it to her garter belt by way of a satiny elastic strap.

Though his expression never changed, his crystal blue eyes took on a smoky hue that pulled at memories long suppressed. Then his hands were gone, and Sunny struggled to drag in a shaky breath.

The guests clapped and cheered. Kirk stood and offered Sunny his hand. She rose on wobbly legs, keenly aware of the lace garter encircling her thigh, and the lingering imprint of his fingers on the bare skin just above her stocking.

Vaguely she heard the emcee inviting Charli and Grant to join the two of them on the dance floor. The band started playing a slow standard. Kirk took the bouquet from her and lobbed it to Amanda, standing on the sidelines. He pulled Sunny into his arms, and they started moving to the music. He was bigger, taller, more solid than she remembered, but one thing hadn't changed. His scent, the clean, masculine essence of his skin, was the same.

Sunny was reminded of the first time they'd made love all those years ago, when Kirk's parents had spent the weekend in Cambridge, Massachusetts, having driven his older sister to Harvard. The scent of Kirk had been an aphrodisiac as she'd lain naked with him on his narrow twin bed, nuzzling his hair, his throat, his chest, burning with adolescent passion, dizzy with anticipation, aching with love for the golden youth she'd lost her heart to.

Sunny closed her eyes for one brief moment and inhaled deeply. *Don't do this to yourself*, she thought. *Stop torturing yourself with memories.* That particular pastime had been pointless twelve years ago, and it was downright destructive now, when she had to focus on her goals. She was thirty years old. Dwelling on the past would not put a husband in her bed or a child in her womb.

They shared the floor with Charli and Grant, the newlyweds holding each other close, sharing secret smiles and private whispers.

"Some reunion, huh?" Kirk asked. His warm breath stirred the loose hairs springing free at Sunny's temple.

She looked up at him. "Is that what this is? A reunion?"

"I'd say when you haven't seen someone in over a decade, it qualifies as a reunion." When she didn't respond, he added, "It was nice of Charli to invite me at the last minute. I just got into town yesterday."

Sunny forced a smile. "So. You're a daddy."

Kirk's expression softened. "His name's Ian. He's eighteen months old." He smoothly steered them away from the other couples now drifting onto the dance floor.

"Um...I knew you were teaching physics out there at Stanford. I didn't know you'd gotten married."

"Three years ago." He glanced away for a moment; his fingers tightened around hers. "Linda died in a car accident on New Year's Day."

Sunny's chest constricted painfully. "Oh, Kirk... I'm so sorry."

He said nothing. She felt stiff and awkward, wishing suddenly that they were someplace quiet and private.

Kirk's voice was strained. "I stuck it out at Stanford till the end of the school year. Now I'm home for good. *We're* home, Ian and me."

Home for good? Sunny searched his eyes. "You mean...you're moving back here? To Long Island?"

He nodded. "This is where I belong. I was thinking of moving back a few years ago, and then I met Linda, and, well, those plans got shelved. When I lost her I realized it was time to come home. Ian will be near his grandparents, his aunts and uncles and cousins...."

The bleakness in his eyes grabbed hold of Sunny's heart and squeezed.

He added, "It won't be like having his mom back, but it'll be good for him, having his whole extended family nearby."

Sunny nodded, at a loss for words. Amanda, dancing past with one of Charli's many brothers, caught her eye and winked. Did Sunny's Wedding Ring pals know about Kirk's marriage and the death of his wife?

They had to, she realized. None of them had seemed surprised when he'd mentioned his son. Raven had described Kirk as lighthearted and buoyant. Clearly she was remembering him the way he'd been in high school, when he hadn't a care in the world aside from fixing up his vintage Jaguar. The man Sunny was dancing with was not that same carefree youth.

She said, "Something tells me you wouldn't have moved back here without lining up a job first."

"I'll be teaching at Garrison in the fall." Garrison University, a renowned research institution, occupied a sprawling campus on Long Island's South Shore. "What about you?"

"What *about* me?" She averted her eyes, already feeling a prickle of embarrassment.

"What have you been doing with yourself?" he asked. After a moment of silence he added, "Still single, I assume, since you caught the bouquet."

"Yep. Still single."

When she didn't elaborate, he asked, "So what are you up to nowadays?"

"Same thing I was up to last time we saw each other."

He chuckled. "Right. Serving the He-Man Special at Wafflemania. Seriously. What do you do for a living?"

Sunny kept her gaze directed at the band as she said, "That's what I've been doing, Kirk. Seriously."

He was silent for long, agonizing seconds as the merriment around them continued unabated. "Listen," he said quietly, "I didn't mean to make it sound..."

Sunny pasted on a smile. She forced herself to meet his chagrined gaze. "Sure you did. Don't worry, I'm used to it. I fill an important function in my social crowd. I'm the resident underachiever. My job is to make all my friends feel good about their lives."

"Sunny—"

"I mean, there's Raven, a successful hypnotherapist, with her own practice and everything. And Charli, teaching instrumental music at our old high school. And look at Amanda. Publisher of a children's magazine! Rewarding, well-respected careers, all of them. And then there's Sunny. No drive. No ambition. Whenever the others are feeling crappy about their lives, all they have to do is look at me and—"

"Sunny, stop it." Kirk's body radiated tension, even as he continued to lead her around the dance floor.

"I'm just telling it like it is."

He took a deep breath. He glanced around at the couples dancing nearby and lowered his voice. "What happened? You started working at that greasy-spoon joint right after graduation. For some quick cash, I figured. I never thought it would last."

Neither did I. "What can I tell you? I've discovered the smell of grilled burgers is a real turn-on."

"That's not the kind of job you make a career out of. Not *you*."

"Hey, we can't all be hotshot college professors with our name splashed all over the physics journals."

"You know, this is something you used to do. Bluster your way out of it when you felt defensive or embarrassed."

"Sounds like you missed your calling, Dr. Larsen. Maybe you should've gone into psychology."

"It won't work, Sunny. I want an answer. What the hell happened? You had so much promise."

Sunny swallowed hard. "What I do is good honest work, Kirk. It's nothing to be ashamed of."

"I never said it was. I'm sorry if that's how I came across. I'm just...confused. I figured you'd take a year to get your act together, accumulate a little money. And then you'd go to college, get some kind of liberal arts degree. Maybe become a teacher. You always loved kids."

The song ended and the band struck up a livelier tune. Sunny was relieved when Kirk took her hand

and drew her off the dance floor, and surprised when he headed straight for the exit. Raven caught Sunny's eye as they passed her table. Sunny felt as if she were under a microscope, every detail of this "reunion" with Kirk analyzed and overanalyzed by her well-meaning Wedding Ring friends.

Kirk didn't stop until they were outside the elegant catering establishment, located within a huge county park. It was nearly 10:00 p.m., a balmy night in early July. A parking attendant approached. Kirk waved him away and led Sunny under the colonnade and past the lit fountain to a wooden bench nestled in a grouping of giant boxwoods strung with tiny white lights. There they sat, listening to the muted sounds of revelry from within the building, inhaling the summer-scented breeze.

The minutes stretched on. Kirk leaned back against the bench, and Sunny felt a bit of the tension drain from him. She sensed that he didn't often let himself relax. She stared at his profile by moonlight, the strong jaw, the steep, high-bridged nose that had always put her in mind of a Roman emperor. Or a Viking, now, with the long hair and grim expression. No, not grim, she thought. Melancholy. When did he say his wife had died? New Year's Day. Six months ago.

How crushing it must have been, to lose her so suddenly like that. His life partner. The mother of his child. Sunny did some quick mental arithmetic. Ian had only been a year old when it happened. Had his mother gotten to see him blow out his first birthday candle?

That was perhaps the saddest part, Sunny thought. Kirk's son wouldn't remember his mother; he was just too young.

Automatically her hand moved to cover Kirk's, where it rested on his thigh, but she stopped herself.

"I was out of line before." He sounded weary. "It's none of my business what you do with your life."

His words settled like a deadweight in Sunny's chest. There'd been a time when everything about her had been very much his business, when the two of them had been hopelessly in love and completely wrapped up in each other's lives.

How could she explain twelve years wiping coffee and syrup off Formica diner tables, while pocketing her measly tips? Twelve long years with her life on hold, waiting for her soul mate, whoever he might be, to stroll through the doors of Wafflemania and order the He-Man Special with one eager bride to go.

No. She couldn't share that with him. Not Kirk. Better that he think he'd misjudged her all those years ago, that youthful ardor had caused him to see promise in her where there was none.

He lifted a strand of her hair and drew it slowly through his fingers. He twisted the end around his fingertip and watched the waves spring back when he released it. For the longest time he didn't meet her eyes. A fluttery sensation rose in Sunny's throat.

She *could* still read him. It may have been a dozen

years since she'd set eyes on Kirk, but there was still something there, a connection, albeit frayed.

"I've thought about you," he said, staring off into the inky blackness of the woods. Sighing, he loosened his necktie and undid the top button of his pale blue dress shirt. "A lot. Too much." He looked at her then. "Don't misunderstand me. I loved Linda."

"I know you did."

He searched her face. "How could you know that?"

"I know *you*, Kirk. For you to marry someone, make a life with her, make—" Sunny's voice cracked "—make a child with her, well, I just know you had to really be in love. You're...you're the most sincere guy I ever knew."

He stared at her for long moments, while crickets trilled and a trio of guests exited the building, laughing. "People change," he said. "Maybe I'm not the same sincere guy you remember."

She tilted her head, studying him. "You *have* changed. It's been twelve years. You've been through a lot. But deep inside..." She laid her hand on his chest, over the strong, steady beat of his heart. "You're still you."

Slowly Kirk lifted her hand from his chest, wrapped his long fingers around hers. Absently he brushed his lips over her knuckles, side to side. It was a gesture she remembered well; he used to do it when he was deep in thought. Had he done it with Linda?

Finally he spoke. "Are you involved with any-one?"

There it was. Sunny's head reeled with conflicting emotions. She'd been bushwhacked by her best friends, when she'd least expected it. It was too soon. She needed time: time to think this through, to decide how she felt about getting involved with Kirk again, after...everything.

When she didn't answer, he said quietly, "Can I assume that's a yes?"

"No. I'm..." She cleared her throat. "I'm not involved with anyone."

He settled their linked hands on his thigh and rubbed his thumb across her palm. "I'd like to see you again, Sunny."

Under the terms of the Wedding Ring pact, she was now officially obligated to date him—for at least three months unless he broke it off sooner. She had no choice in the matter, and she couldn't decide whether to be outraged by that—by her friends' presumptuousness in choosing this man of all men for her—or relieved. The decision, after all, was now out of her hands. She didn't have to analyze it, to weigh the pros and cons. Her lifelong pals, who supposedly knew her better than anyone and knew what, and who, she needed, had already done that for her.

Lightly he squeezed her hand. "There hasn't been anyone since Linda. It was all I could do to...well, getting involved with someone else has been the furthest thing from my mind. But when I saw you in there..." He trailed off.

"You don't think maybe it's just that you, well, feel comfortable with me? I mean, I'm someone from your past. In a sense, I must represent the 'good old days.'"

He smiled wryly. "You mean, is this just a pathetic effort to recreate happier times?" He seemed to ponder that a moment. "Maybe it is, Sunny. I won't pretend to know my own mind at this point. I haven't been thinking straight since..." He released her hand and leaned forward, elbows on knees, head cradled in his palms. After a moment he dragged his fingers through his hair.

"You're right," he said, standing. "This is premature."

"I didn't mean..." What did she mean? Here was her out. He was backpedaling, and it would be easy enough to shut up and let him. "Nice try," she'd tell Amanda and Raven and Charli, "but he's not interested. So that's that. Find me another guy."

And they would. They'd find her someone new, made of all-new materials. No recycled emotions. No threadbare psychological baggage. No good old days.

Kirk turned and started toward the building. He was almost there when Sunny called, "Kirk?"

He turned and looked at her, a tall, almost spectral presence, his pale suit and hair suffused with silvery moonlight.

Sunny realized she no more knew her mind than did Kirk. All she knew was that if she let him walk away...

"I'd like to see you, too." She stood. Her thigh tingled where the bridal garter hugged it. "If you still want to."

Kirk stood staring at her, his expression unreadable. Finally he lifted his hand to her. Sunny closed the distance on unsteady legs and twined her fingers with his.

2

"JUST TELL ME YOU DIDN'T turn vegetarian on me."

Kirk looked up from where he sat cross-legged on the floor of his new office, surrounded by cartons of books and files, to see Sunny leaning in the doorway.

He couldn't ignore the rush of pleasure he experienced at the sight of her standing there in her short white sundress and floppy straw hat, wagging a wicker picnic basket at him, even as he asked himself, for the hundredth time, what the hell he was doing.

It's too soon. Isn't it? Linda had always said that if "something happened" to her, she'd want him to get on with his life; she'd want him to find someone else and be happy.

That was what she'd said, but he'd never really believed her. He'd never given it much thought, actually, except in the most abstract sense. Not when she was alive, anyway.

Kirk nodded toward the old-fashioned picnic hamper. "I didn't think people really used those. Don't you have to be in a feminine hygiene commercial or something to carry a basket like that?"

"Beats a plastic cooler for charm any day." Sunny

ambled into his office, glancing around at the functional furnishings, the row of framed diplomas propped against one wall, awaiting picture hooks. "I found it on one of those home-shopping channels. A steal at twenty-nine ninety-five. Check it out." She flipped open the basket's hinged double lid and gestured expansively. "It came with everything you see here."

"All that food?"

"The food, no. The sixteen-piece set of picnicware in durable, festively colored melamine, yes."

Kirk shoved a file into the open credenza, slammed it closed and rose to his feet. "Home-shopping channel, huh? I've never ordered anything off TV myself."

"Don't tell me. You surf past the Diamonique baubles with all due haste on your way to the more intellectually demanding channels. Discovery, History, Learning..."

"When I can find time for the boob tube at all, it's either ESPN or one of the movie channels. And to answer your question—" Kirk took the surprisingly heavy basket from Sunny and peered into it "—I still eat meat. What's on the menu?"

"Roast beef sandwiches, potato salad, iced tea and apple pie. Oh, and some Waldorf salad left over from last night's dinner."

"Everything homemade, I assume."

She smiled. "I still like to cook."

Sunny's mother had gone back to work as a day-care teacher when her youngest child, Sunny's sister Samantha, entered junior high. All four siblings had been assigned chores. Sunny, the oldest, cooked dinner each night. She loved to cook, but she hated to run to the grocery store for ingredients that weren't on hand. Thus her culinary policy of "imaginative substitution," which resulted in some interesting meals.

The Bleecker household was laid-back, and the kids' friends were always welcome at the dinner table. Kirk had broken bread countless times with his girlfriend and her family. Those were good memories, full of warmth and laughter and stimulating conversation.

Perhaps Sunny was right, Kirk mused. Perhaps his impulse to renew their relationship was a retreat into the comforting refuge of the past, a time when his world was rock-solid and his biggest quandary was deciding whether to go to Stanford or Caltech.

"Let's get out of here." He laid a palm on Sunny's back and ushered her into the third-floor hallway of Garrison University's physics building. "I've been holed up in this place for so long, I'm going stir-crazy."

KIRK LOUNGED ON HIS SIDE on the picnic blanket Sunny had brought—a handmade quilt that had seen better days—and watched her toss a Frisbee with a couple of shirtless college students and a chocolate Labrador retriever sporting a yellow bandanna around its neck. Kirk and Sunny had settled in a grassy field near one of the campus's dormitory complexes and polished off the picnic lunch in short order. When the Frisbee had landed in Kirk's potato salad, he'd whipped it back like a pro, and the guys had asked him to join the game. He'd declined, an automatic response, but Sunny had jumped up, shed her sandals and hat and invited herself to play.

The guys had exchanged a look. Clearly they hadn't bargained on this. A female—particularly one of Sunny's advanced years—was bound to put a damper on their fast-paced game.

But they hadn't counted on this particular geriatric female. She sprinted after the blue plastic disk with seemingly inexhaustible energy, breasts bouncing, long hair flying, the Lab barking at her heels. Each time she leaped to catch a high throw, the hem of her short dress flipped up, revealing the entire length of her bare, suntanned legs and, every so often, a glimpse of floral-printed panties. Her keen-eyed fellow Frisbee-tossers, meanwhile, appeared to suffer a lapse in concentration, causing them to fumble their catches more often than not. Far from resenting her participation, they began to throw it to her at every opportunity, their aim suspiciously high.

Observing Sunny's unrestrained exuberance as she wrestled the dog for possession of the Frisbee and hurled it through the air with more enthusiasm than skill, Kirk didn't have to ask himself why he hadn't even considered joining them. The reason was part and parcel of why he suspected that even this innocent outing—a picnic with his high school sweetheart—was a monumental mistake.

Sunny finally quit the game, to the grumbling disappointment of her new pals, and flopped onto her back on the quilt. The Lab trotted along behind her, displaying an interest in the contents of the picnic hamper. A sharp whistle from his master sent him tearing off across the field.

"Whew! That was fun." Sunny fanned herself with her hat. She smacked Kirk playfully. "You should've joined us. What's the matter, Professor? Too dignified to work up a sweat with underclassmen?"

She was breathing hard, her cheeks flushed. The sun glinted like fire in the auburn waves spread out on the quilt, and turned her violet eyes to glowing amethysts. Kirk leaned on an elbow over her. The prospect of working up a sweat held an undeniable appeal at the moment, but underclassmen were not part of the equation.

The jolt of sexual desire stunned him. For months his libido had lain dormant, suppressed along with all other human feelings under the crushing weight of his loss. It felt more like apathy than true depression, as if everything in his life had gone flat. Whether the cause was his grief over losing Linda or his overwhelming feelings of inadequacy as a single parent, or some combination of the two, he couldn't say.

Yet here was this woman from his past, his first love, making him feel like a horny eighteen-year-old.

"Hey, I know!" she said. "You could've turned it into a physics lesson for those kids—the aerodynamics of the Frisbee! What're they doing on campus in July, anyway? Do they have summer school or something?"

"Some courses are offered during the summer, but the students could also be working on campus, or just hanging out." Kirk reached over Sunny to snatch the last bit of piecrust she'd left on her plate. As he did so, his forearm brushed her breasts, warm and resilient under the cotton sundress. His skin seemed to tighten all over for one long, breathless moment as he avoided her eyes.

He polished off the rich piecrust, watching the Frisbee players—while Sunny watched him. He sensed her amethyst gaze like a caress. Finally she spoke.

"I'd like to meet Ian."

Kirk looked at her, at the open, guileless expression that held nothing back. He let out a long breath.

"I don't think that's a good idea."

She stared at him unblinking for an instant, before her gaze skittered away.

"What I mean is..." Kirk sighed. "He's at a...a vulnerable point right now. Moving from California, bonding with his grandparents. I don't want to, well, throw too many new people at him at once."

"You don't want him bonding with the wrong person."

"Sunny..."

"It's all right." She sat up and smoothed her dress. "If I had a child, I'd be protective of him, too." She cast a smile his way, but it looked forced.

Kirk's fingers clenched. "The truth is, I don't know what's right for him. I'm doing my best, but there's no blueprint for this, for how to cope with..." He raised his hand and let it fall. "Maybe this was all a mistake, this move back home. Maybe I should've stayed put, stayed on at Stanford for another year at least, waited for the dust to settle before uprooting him."

"You trusted your gut. There's nothing wrong with that, Kirk."

"They say you shouldn't make important decisions right on the heels of...something like this. You're supposed to wait until you can think with a clear head. But I just had this overwhelming urge to bolt—that's the only way I can describe it. Linda was gone and nothing was going to change that, and for me to stay out there, where we'd built a life, in the house we'd found together, fixed up together..." He shook his head again. "I couldn't bear the thought of it. I just had to get away, as fast as possible."

"It isn't as if you didn't have your reasons," Sunny said. "Didn't you tell me you wanted Ian to be near his relatives, to have the love and support of his extended family? Made sense to me. It still does.

Kirk..." She lifted her hand. He felt her cool fingers on the back of his neck, over the edge of his charcoal-gray T-shirt. "It's normal to doubt yourself after what you've been through. But you don't have to let it eat you up."

When he didn't answer, she said, "I know. Who am I to talk, right? What do I know about losing a spouse?"

"That's not it. I know you mean well, but, Sunny...I'm not the same idealistic guy you knew way back when. You need to know that."

Her smile was bittersweet. "Well, I hope this doesn't come as too much of a shock, but I'm not the same dewy-eyed girl, either. I haven't experienced the kind of tragedy you have, but believe me, I've gone through my own changes."

There was an edge to her voice Kirk hadn't heard before. He tilted his head and studied her. "What happened?"

She dropped her hand. Her expression hardened. "I grew up. Stopped believing in fairy tales."

"What kind of fairy tales might those be?"

She started to speak, and stopped herself. "It's not important."

"To whom? Come on, let's have it."

She shrugged. "You know, just the usual school-girl fantasies. The kind of unrealistic dreams most women outgrow in time to make something of their lives."

He hesitated. "Are we talking about the knight-in-shining-armor type of fantasies? Mr. Right?"

She averted her gaze. After an awkward silence she said, "You wanted to know why I never continued my education, why I stayed with my stupid dead-end job for so long."

"I never said it was a—"

She gave him a quelling look. "I know what you said. And you were right. I've wasted my life waiting for that knight in shining armor."

Gently he said, "Don't you think you're overstating it a bit?"

"Am I? I saw the look in your eyes when you found out I was still waiting tables at Wafflemania."

"I guess the thing I don't get is...someone can go to college, fulfill their potential, have a rewarding career and all that—and still find their soul mate. *I* did."

"It's different for men. You must know that. I want children, Kirk, a houseful of them, and there's no way I'll let them be raised by baby-sitters. Settling down with a good man and raising a family—it's all I've ever wanted. You know the kind of big, loving household I grew up in. To me, that's the cornerstone of a happy life. That *is* fulfilling my potential. Everything else, career and all that, it's all secondary. I guess I just didn't see the point in going to college, wasting all that time and money...."

"When marriage and full-time motherhood were in your future."

"Needless to say—" Sunny gave a casual head toss that didn't fool Kirk for a second "—my grand plans of happily-ever-after never got past the daydream phase. The blushing groom failed to materialize. Nowadays if you can even track down a stable, employed, heterosexual man who doesn't run screaming at the mention of marriage, he's not likely to look twice at a thirtyish waitress who spends her evenings soaking her feet and scrubbing egg stains out of a Pepto Bismol-colored polyester uniform. Trust me on this one."

Kirk didn't say what he was thinking, which was that the kind of man who fueled Sunny's happily-ever-after fantasies was probably looking for a woman with interests and aspirations of her own, a woman whose personal fulfillment wasn't limited to him and their marriage. It sounded like she'd already discovered that the hard way.

She finished repacking the picnic basket in silence. Finally she closed the top and sat staring at it for long moments. At last she looked up at him, her expression solemn. "What happened to us, Kirk?"

He frowned. "What, you mean...back in high school?"

She nodded.

He shrugged. "I went to California. To Stanford." When she said nothing, he added, "I did suggest you apply to some schools out there, as I recall."

Sunny was a good student, but they'd both known

she had little hope of getting into elite Stanford University. But there were plenty of other good colleges out there that she could have gone to.

"Yeah," she said listlessly. "You did. And I told you I wasn't ready for college."

He drew in a slow breath. "I know you wanted to just move out there with me."

She'd never said it in so many words, back then. She'd waited for him to ask her to join him in California.

To get married as soon as possible.

Only, he never did. The subject had throbbed between them, unspoken, for months.

"You figured I'd just be in the way," she said tightly. "There was a whole new life waiting for you out there, all those college girls…"

"That's not true. You meant more to me than…" Helplessly Kirk shook his head. "Don't you see, we couldn't have done it that way. I was still just a kid, dependent on my folks for tuition, living expenses, everything. How could I take on the responsibility for someone else?"

"I would've *worked!*" she cried. "What, you think I intended to sponge off you and your parents?"

"No, of course not—that's not your way. It just would've been so unrealistic. I thought you'd have figured that out by now."

"What can I say? I'm dense."

"Sunny…"

"What was so unrealistic? You going to school, me working, until we could afford a place of our own. Other people have done it."

Kirk rubbed his forehead. "I was facing this grueling course of study. I needed all my concentration. That was my priority. You make it sound so easy, but I *would've* felt responsible for you if you'd followed me out there."

Sunny's spine straightened. "Is that how you saw it, Kirk? Me 'following' you to California? You make me sound like some kind of—of stray mutt that you couldn't shake."

"That's not fair. You're the one who made the decision to stay here and wait tables. I asked you to apply to schools out there. We could've been together—"

"I told you why college wasn't right for me."

"If you'd believed in us, you would've done it. You'd have seen that it was the only way for us to—"

"If *I'd* believed in us?" Sunny's eyes glittered with righteous indignation. "*You* left *me*, Kirk! You could've gone to Columbia, right here in New York—maybe an hour and a half away by train and subway. Even if you'd gone to Harvard or MIT, we're talking three or four hours max on Amtrak. Same with Johns Hopkins in Baltimore. They're all wonderful schools. But no, you had to go to California."

"Stanford and Caltech happened to be my top choices. It had nothing to do with you."

"Yeah, I already figured that out."

"No, I mean..." Kirk rubbed his forehead. The hell with it. She knew what he meant. "Dammit, Sunny, why bring this up now? Why now, after twelve years? It's not like we can go back in time, undo the choices we made."

Her chin wobbled. She averted her eyes, and Kirk realized with shock that she was close to tears. He sat paralyzed for several moments, before gently turning her and pulling her into his arms.

"Sunny..." He cradled her against his chest, tucked her head under his chin. The feel of her, all warmth and feminine softness, kindled memories long banked. Her silky hair teased the skin of his throat. He dipped his head and pressed a kiss to the crown of her head, breathing deeply of her subtle scent, part citrus, part musk, one hundred percent Sunny. Pressed so closely to her, he felt every shaky breath as she struggled to govern her emotions.

He murmured, "The fact is, we both have to answer for what happened twelve years ago. If I *could* go back and undo my choices..." Without warning, Linda's face sprang to mind. He pictured her the way she'd looked on their wedding day, glowing with a radiant happiness that he'd shared. And then a year and a half later, her lovely face flushed and contorted as she'd clenched his hand with bone-cracking force, laboring to bring their child into the world. His own helpless anxiety had turned to awe-struck jubilation as he'd glimpsed his newborn son's pink, wrinkled face, heard his shrill, toothless howl of indignation. That precious little face, the eyes and mouth so like his mother's.

Sunny raised her glistening eyes to his. "Don't be silly. Of course you wouldn't undo your choices," she said with a tender, all-knowing smile, and for the first time in six months, Kirk felt his heart swell in a flood of drenching warmth. He closed his eyes against the stinging purity of it.

To care again—about anything in life, about any-*one* except his son. He wasn't sure he was up to it.

He felt Sunny's smooth fingers on his cheek, felt her turn in his arms to face him. He opened his eyes to see her staring up at him with such candid affection it was as if the clock had indeed been turned back, as if their soul-deep connection had never been interrupted. As if he harbored no secrets from this woman.

In that enchanted instant, Kirk wished it were true. Sunny didn't know everything about him, and if she did...

No. It was too soon. He couldn't risk it. Not when this woman had it within her power to lift the pall he'd been living under for half a year, to pull him back into the light, to make him care again, to make him *feel* again.

A frightening prospect, but for the first time since those two cops had rung his doorbell last New Year's Day, Kirk allowed himself to wonder how it would feel to be whole again. He sent out mental feelers, probing his rawest wounds. The pain was still there, but so was a glimmering thread of hope.

"It's true what I said the other day. I've thought about you." Kirk cupped her face in his hands. "A lot."

Sunny wore a wry smile. "I've thought about you, too. More than a lot. I've never felt the same way about...about anyone else." She looked embarrassed. "I wasn't going to tell you that."

The warmth in Kirk's chest burned hotter as he lowered his head and touched his lips to Sunny's. She started, just a bit, at the feather-soft contact. Her eyes closed and he inhaled her whispery sigh.

It wasn't enough. God help him, at that moment he knew he could never get enough of this extraordinary woman. He tucked her more firmly into his embrace, tilting her head, deepening the kiss. It was as if it were all new to him, as if he'd never before held a woman, touched a woman, his senses heightened to the utmost extreme.

Sunny slid her arms around him, and a groan rumbled up Kirk's throat. Suddenly he was back in his boyhood room that weekend his folks had taken his sister Anne to Harvard, and Sunny was there with him, and they were going to do it, at last, after endless months of dating and yearning and sweaty back seat groping. They'd undressed each other with awkward eagerness, twisting the sheets into a hopeless tangle at the foot of his bed.

U2's poignant song "With or Without You" had

pulsed from his stereo's speakers as he'd joined his
virgin body with hers, overwhelmed by the irrefut-
able rightness of it, by the startling slippery heat that
both eased his entry and spurred him on. She'd
gasped and clung and lifted to him as he'd breached
her narrow opening, her expression awestruck.

And here she was in his arms once more, on a sun-
warmed quilt under a dazzling summer sky, and
some part of him knew it was right again, so right.

They parted, breathless. Kirk looked down into
Sunny's flushed face, her eyes drowsy with desire,
her lips moist and swollen.

"We can be at my place in ten minutes," he whispered hoarsely, and pressed hard, fast kisses to her
temple, her cheekbone, her mouth. "Come on." He
leaped up from the quilt and grabbed the picnic basket.

Sunny didn't move. "What about Ian?"

"My folks have him till three." He tugged a corner
of the quilt, urging her to rise, to no avail. "What?"

"It's...it's too soon."

"Too soon? Sunny, it's not like we're a couple of
kids anymore. It's not like we've never made love."

"Shh!" She glanced toward the Frisbee players,
though they were too far away to hear.

Squatting in front of her, Kirk said quietly, "It
doesn't feel too soon to me, Sunny. It feels like...like
this is what I've been waiting for. Like *you're* what
I've been waiting for."

She sighed, clearly torn. He stroked her face cajolingly, brushed his thumb over her lips. She pressed her hand over his and turned her head to kiss his palm. She didn't look at him as she said, "I don't know if you're really that ready, Kirk."

He was about to laughingly refute her statement— he'd never been more ready!—but in the next heartbeat her meaning sank in, and the words died on his tongue. He was ready to sleep with her, she was saying, but not ready to introduce her to his son. Knowing that any attempt to rationalize the unintentional insult would only compound it, he simply rose and offered his hand. She blinked up at him for a moment, with the sun in her eyes, before allowing him to help her up.

They were halfway to the physics building before he spoke. "Like I said, I'm still trying to figure all this out. Including what's best for Ian." With a self-deprecating smirk he added, "How patient are you?"

Sunny slipped her arm through his. "How does three months sound?"

"Three months?" His brow wrinkled. "How did you come up with three months?"

With a secret little smile she said, "Maybe someday you'll find out."

3

"WITH BLUEBERRY SYRUP." Five-year-old David MacLeod handed his vinyl-bound menu to Sunny.

"I know. And grapefruit juice." Sunny jotted the notation on her order pad.

"How'd you know?" Davey demanded.

His father laughed. "I think Sunny knows your preferences by now, Son."

The MacLeods had been regulars at Wafflemania since shortly after little Davey's birth. They showed up every Sunday after church. A creature of habit, the tyke never deviated from his standard brunch order of a Belgian waffle and sausage links drowned in gallons of blueberry syrup, with a grapefruit-juice chaser.

Emily MacLeod tucked a paper napkin into the collar of her son's white oxford-cloth shirt. When he objected she patiently explained, "When you're big enough to eat your breakfast without getting syrup all over yourself, you won't need a bib."

"I'm big enough!" Davey tore the napkin off. "I don't want a dumb baby bib!"

"Another stained shirt," Emily sighed. With a defeated little smile she added, "If only it weren't *blue-berry* syrup."

"May I?" Jim MacLeod casually commandeered the discarded napkin and tucked it into his own collar.

Davey gaped at his dad. "*You* don't wear a bib!"

Jim spared his son a glance. "Sometimes I do. Remember those lobsters we ate at Aunt Irene's?"

Davey's sucking thumb drifted toward his mouth as he gravely pondered this latest development. At the last instant his newly honed big-boy reflexes kicked in and he jerked his thumb away from his face. This time when his mother offered him a napkin, he jammed it in his collar himself, carefully fanning it over his shirt exactly as his dad had done.

Sunny chewed back a grin. "I'll go get your juice." She looked forward to the MacLeods' weekly visits. To her they represented the ideal family, straight out of a Norman Rockwell painting. Emily and Jim were obviously good parents, patient and loving, and just as obviously devoted to each other. They practically oozed family harmony. Not that Sunny was naive. She assumed that the MacLeods, like all couples, had their occasional marital tiffs and moments of frustration in raising their rambunctious son, but observing them week after week, year after year, she couldn't help thinking of them as the quintessential happy family.

Being around the MacLeods always boosted Sunny's spirits, but it also made her wistful. This young family represented the very goals and dreams that had eluded Sunny herself for so long. Every time she saw Emily MacLeod hug her son or even wipe his face, with that doting, maternal smile she reserved just for him, Sunny's eyes stung. Her empty arms ached for a warm little body to cuddle.

Would she ever know that kind of fulfillment? Was the simple joy of having a husband and children too much to ask for?

Perhaps Kirk was right. Perhaps she'd gone about attaining her goal the wrong way. She'd installed herself in a dead-end job in her sleepy hometown, passively waiting for some faceless knight in shining armor to discover her and sweep her off her feet. Meanwhile she'd done little to enrich her life, to "fulfill her potential," in Kirk's words, to make herself into the kind of intriguing damsel who could not only catch the knight's eye, but keep his interest over the long haul.

She and Kirk had seen each other several times in the eleven days since their picnic at the university. They'd spent a Wednesday evening at Hunter's comedy club, Stitches. There they'd enjoyed scrumptious pan pizzas and a string of amateur comics that included Hunter's wife, Raven, who regaled them with a hilarious routine about pregnancy and morning sickness. A few days later Kirk and Sunny had spent a leisurely afternoon wandering around Chinatown and Little Italy in downtown Manhattan.

And just last Tuesday he'd taken her to Island Park, where they'd rented a motorboat to fish for fluke.

Sunny returned to the MacLeods' table with Davey's juice and syrup, then moved on to the smoking section to pour coffee for a party of six hefty high-school football jocks who had managed to squeeze into a booth. Behind her she heard Fran, the hostess, say, "Just the two of you? Smoking or nonsmoking?"

A familiar deep voice answered, "We can't stay. We just popped in to say hi to someone."

Sunny wheeled around to see Kirk standing near the entrance, wearing a white polo shirt and khaki shorts. In his arms was a squirming towheaded toddler, craning his little neck to get a better look at the dessert case.

Sunny's heart thumped hard, nearly knocking her off balance.

Ian.

This had to be Kirk's little boy. Her assumption was confirmed when the child strained toward the beguiling array of desserts, crying, "Okkie! Da, okkie!"

"Yes, I see the cookies, Ian. And cakes and pies and—"

"Wan' okkie!"

Trying to hush his son, Kirk scanned the room for Sunny, casting her an apologetic smile when he spotted her. As if Ian were the first loud, cookie-crazed toddler Wafflemania had ever seen!

Sunny slipped her order pad into her pocket and smoothed the short skirt of her blindingly pink uniform as she made her way toward them. Since he'd come home, Kirk had never seen her here at the diner, in the tacky outfit she was obliged to wear, right down to the shiny support hose and white Reeboks. She was embarrassed to have him see her like this, and angry at herself for being embarrassed.

As she joined them, Kirk's crystal-blue eyes glowed with affection—and something else. Nervous anticipation perhaps. He didn't kiss Sunny hello, as was his custom, but swiveled his body in an attempt to divert his son's attention from the goodies. It didn't work.

"Ian," Kirk said, "I have someone I want you to meet." He ruffled the child's pale hair, urging him to acknowledge Sunny. Ian didn't even glance at her, his attention riveted to the brightly lit dessert case.

"Okkie!" The demand was now a frustrated whine. "Da! Okkie!"

"You'd think he was starving," Kirk said. "You'd never know he just scarfed down an adult-size slice of pizza."

"Then this sounds like a good time for dessert." Sunny scooted behind the counter, then paused in the process of opening the case. "If it's all right with Daddy?"

"It's all right with Daddy." Kirk chuckled.

Ian watched, transfixed, as Sunny slid out the tray

of assorted jumbo cookies. "Which one would you like?" she asked the toddler.

His finger shot toward a cookie studded with colorful M&M's.

"Good choice. That's my favorite, too." Sunny handed it to him along with a paper napkin.

"Say 'thank you,'" Kirk instructed.

Crumbs sprayed from Ian's mouth as he parroted, "Ank-oo."

"You're very welcome."

Kirk mouthed his own thanks as she returned the cookies to the case. "This nice lady is named Sunny," he told the boy. "She's a friend of mine."

Ian stared at Sunny as he gnawed on his prize.

She said, "I hope you and I will be friends, too, Ian."

Sunny's boss, Mike, from his perch on a stool behind the cash register, caught her eye and jerked his head toward the busy dining room.

"Yeah, yeah," she muttered.

"I didn't mean to get you in trouble," Kirk said.

"Oh, don't worry about that old blowhard. He's all bark." Unable to help herself, Sunny reached out to stroke Ian's warm little back through his Disneyland T-shirt—and was blindsided by a wave of maternal longing so intense it stole her breath. Dropping her hand, she averted her face for a moment, pretending to check on her customers.

She could give this darling little boy a half brother or sister. Maybe a whole passel of them. The thought ambushed her from out of nowhere. She shouldn't be thinking along those lines. It was premature.

But once planted, the idea stuck like a burr. She imagined herself growing round with Kirk's child, imagined a pregnant belly straining her snug polyester uniform.

"What's so funny?" Kirk asked.

She shook her head, chuckling. "Nothing. I'm just so happy to meet this little cookie snatcher." She tugged playfully on Ian's ear, coaxing a giggle out of him. Now it was her turn to mouth a heartfelt thank-you to Kirk.

His tender smile told her that no thanks were necessary, that the meeting had been overdue.

"Well." He addressed his son. "Are you going to get crumbs all over the back seat of the car?"

Ian nodded vigorously.

"Hey, that's his *job*," Sunny said, giving the boy's back one last loving pat. "Thank you for coming by to meet me, Ian. You made my day much brighter."

"We also came by to ask you to dinner," Kirk said.

"Dinner?"

"Tonight. I'm making spaghetti."

"'Agetti!" Ian squealed in delight.

"Larsen the Younger's personal favorite," Kirk revealed. "And a good thing, too, because it's something Larsen the Elder can actually throw together without messing up too badly."

"I'll bring the ice cream," Sunny said.

"I-keam!" Ian hollered.

She cocked her head at him. "You have a real sweet tooth, don't you, big fella?"

Ian poked his fingers into his mouth—searching for the sweet tooth, she assumed.

Kirk glanced toward the cash register. "Your boss is turning an alarming shade of purple. We'd better let you get back to work before he detonates." Backing toward the doorway, he tossed Sunny a brisk wave, which Ian imitated. "Six o'clock. Make it chocolate chip."

4

KIRK FINISHED DRYING the huge spaghetti pot, part of a set of steel cookware Linda had received at her bridal shower. He tossed the damp dish towel on the countertop as Sunny appeared in the kitchen doorway, thumb raised and sporting a triumphant grin. "Asleep already?" he asked.

"What can I tell you? I've got the touch. Ian was out like a light halfway through 'Scarborough Fair.'"

"You sang him to sleep? *You?*"

One reddish-brown eyebrow lifted. "Your point being?"

"Has your singing voice by any chance, um, undergone some drastic change during the past twelve years?"

"All right, that's it." She snatched up the dish towel he'd abandoned and twirled it menacingly. "Now things are gonna start getting ugly."

Kirk backed up toward the butcher-block island, chuckling as Sunny advanced on him. "Truth hurts, does it?"

"For your information, Larsen the Younger thinks I have a lovely, lilting voice."

Kirk failed to restrain a bark of laughter. "Did you

consider that lapsing into unconsciousness might have been a self-protective mechanism? A way to preserve the poor kid's abused eardrums?"

She mugged outrage while giving the towel a sharp snap aimed at Kirk's midsection. Like a striking cobra, he caught the makeshift weapon and used it to reel her in, banding his arms around her before she had a chance to regroup.

Sunny's eyes sparkled with amusement. "You're still fast."

"One of the advantages of chasing after a toddler." Her breasts, tantalizingly soft and full under her short denim sundress, grazed his chest with each breath she took. He let one hand slide down her back. Slowly, deliberately, he caressed her bottom, his gaze locked with hers. Her lips parted fractionally. Her expressive eyes revealed her uncertainty.

That uncertainty wouldn't last long if Kirk had his way. He brushed his mouth over hers, and felt a little shudder flow through her. "I've missed this." Leaning back against the counter, he kissed her with greater urgency. "I've missed *you*. There was always a part of me no one else could touch."

She melted against him, slipped her arms around him, fitted her body to his as if she were made for him. It felt so good to hold her like this, so sweet and right, he thought he might drown in the perfection of it. That thought fled with all others as he tightened his hold, coaxing her mouth open under his, letting his tongue do what his body craved.

Sunny made a little sound, an imploring whimper, as she met his thrusting tongue with silky strokes of her own. Her fingers fisted in his shirt and she pressed even closer to him, moved her hips with restless sensuality. Kirk couldn't remember ever wanting a woman more. He imagined his tent-pole erection bursting through their clothing, imagined sinking into her welcoming heat in the next two seconds.

He broke the kiss with a growled oath.

"We—we better slow down." Sunny sounded winded. She leaned a little away from him, drawing Kirk's gaze to the front of her dress, to the insistent thrust of her nipples under the pale indigo fabric. He rubbed his thumb over one stiff peak. Her breathing became even more agitated. Her smile was shaky. "That's not—not exactly what I meant by slowing down." She seized his wrist, but made no move to pull him away.

"Slowing down was your idea, not mine." Straightening from the butcher-block island, he captured both nipples between his thumbs and forefingers and gently squeezed them. "You'll have to leave if you want me to stop." Sunny's breasts used to be exquisitely sensitive. They still were, judging by her breathless response. Their lips barely touching, he whispered, "Don't do it."

"Don't what?" She moaned as his touch became bolder, more possessive.

"Don't leave."

The kiss that followed was different from before, more heartfelt than carnal, as if he were pouring his soul into her, saying with his body what he dared not put into words. Not yet.

It might have been a mere two weeks since Kirk had been reunited with Sunny at Charli and Grant's wedding, but there wasn't a doubt in his mind that he needed this warm, sweet, sexy woman in his life.

But did she need him? When she found out about him, as she eventually must, the answer was bound to be a resounding *no*.

How could it be anything else? She'd been up front with him since the beginning, shared her dreams and desires, the deepest yearnings of her heart. And how had he responded? By wooing her, encouraging her to open herself to him, while neatly avoiding the one critical revelation that would surely send her running in the opposite direction.

It was an intentional subterfuge on his part, a lie by omission. But a necessary one. With luck, by the time she found out, she'd be as in love with him as he already knew he was with her, and the truth would have lost its destructive power.

With luck.

They finally came up for air, ending the kiss.

"I feel like I'm eighteen again," she said with a laugh.

"You look like you're eighteen again." He stroked a finger down her warm cheek, now suffused with a pink glow.

She smirked. "Yeah, right. I stopped buying that kind of blatant flattery about the time the checkout boy at the supermarket stopped proofing me for beer. I'm thinking of paying him to start again."

"You're right," he said. "You don't look eighteen."

"Forget it. I'm not paying you, too."

"You're more beautiful now than you were back then. More womanly. More self-confident. It's in your tone of voice, the way you move." His hands drifted down her sides to lightly squeeze her hips. With a wicked grin he added, "Definitely in the way you move."

She recognized his sincerity. He could see it in the shy smile she offered in return.

"Remember Halloween?" he asked.

He didn't need to elaborate. Halloween night of their senior year had been memorable, to say the least. Amanda had thrown a wild costume party at her parents' swanky, sprawling home, attended by about a hundred kids. The consummate hostess even back then, Amanda had outdone herself with incredible food and over-the-top decorations, including yards of spiderweb netting, realistic black bats dangling from the ceiling, and even dry-ice fog. The exterior of the house was just as impressive, with colored lights, a score of candlelit jack-o'-lanterns marching up the porch steps, a front yard full of fake tombstones with humorous epitaphs, a skeleton hanging from a tree by a noose, and even a twenty-foot-high nylon ghost on the roof, lit from within and writhing on a column of pumped air.

The finished basement had been painstakingly converted into a "haunted house," partitioned into a string of small, dark rooms filled with a variety of exhibits, each more hilariously gruesome than the last. Amanda had drafted her closest pals to work the haunted house while the other partygoers filed through, to the accompaniment of recorded moans, shrieks and ghostly wails.

Sunny wore an all-black, skintight bodysuit and head covering adorned with multicolored fluorescent stars. The walls, floor and ceiling of her haunted room sported the same stars on a black background, the only illumination an ultraviolet black light that made the stars glow. Sunny positioned herself in a corner, blending invisibly into the matching background. As her friends passed through in small groups, staring wide-eyed at the room of glowing stars, oblivious to her presence, she leaped out of the corner to scare the snot out of them.

Kirk heard the resulting screams and giddy laughter from his post in the "execution chamber" several rooms away. There he was strapped into what passed for an electric chair, wearing dull prison clothes and a leather hood. He sat perfectly still in the dimly lit room, convincing those passing through that they were looking at a stuffed dummy. He liked to wait until someone jokingly addressed him before pressing the hidden button that activated the sparks and loud sizzling noises. Then all hell broke loose as he bucked violently against the leather restraining straps, howling like a banshee. His audience's reaction had been no less spirited. He was pretty sure Penny Bridgewater had wet herself.

"Which Halloween might that be?" Sunny teased. As if there could be any question.

"Well, I might be referring to the Halloween when you and I were the last ones left in Amanda's haunted basement after everyone else went back upstairs for the costume contest." He slid his hands around her waist.

"Haunted basement?" She feigned confusion. "I'm sorry, I'm drawing a blank."

"Well then, allow me to jog your memory. You were dressed in a star-studded bodysuit, head to toe. I had on this fetching leather ensemble. A bit confining, perhaps."

"I adore men in leather."

"You came looking for me in the execution chamber. I was still strapped to the chair. Arms. Legs. Chest. Nasty-looking hood. Any of this ring a bell?"

"You know, I believe it's beginning to come back to me." Sunny cocked her head as if searching her memory. "Did this hood have tiny little eye slits so you could see?"

"Indeed it did, just like the eye slits in your black hood. I could just make you out in the dim light, this shadowy mass of stars moving into my very limited field of vision."

"I guess everybody forgot you were there."

"Everybody but you."

"Poor thing, tied down to that big, scary chair." Sunny played with the collar of his white polo shirt. "I felt so sorry for you."

"Not sorry enough to untie me, though, huh?"

A devilish little smile played around Sunny's mouth.

"I asked you to. I said, 'Sunny, would you please undo these straps?'"

"It was more like, 'Goddammit, what the hell are you waiting for? Get me out of this thing!'"

Kirk said, "Your memory's improving, I see. Do you remember that you just stood there, not saying a word?"

"I was thinking."

He trailed a fingertip up the long brass zipper that closed the front of her dress. "What were you thinking?"

"I was thinking about how...intriguing you looked, sitting there. A big, strong guy like you, completely at my mercy." She blinked up at him, coy and sultry at the same time. "That's the kind of thing that can give a girl ideas."

"Your first idea, as I recall, was to peel off that bodysuit. Slowly."

Kirk and Sunny had been having sex for two months at that point. They'd only managed a handful of assignations, usually in his bed when his parents were out of the house, and once, out of desperation, in the cramped interior of his twenty-year-old Jaguar. On this Halloween night he'd sat there, bound and helpless, gaping through the leather hood as his girlfriend pulled off her own hood, shook her short curls and proceeded to wriggle out of that sprayed-on outfit. Stunned, he'd asked what she was doing. She'd said nothing.

Kirk said, "My first surprise was that you weren't wearing a bra." Her skin had seemed to glow in the semidark. When her breasts had popped into view, his eyes widened beneath the hood.

"I didn't want lines under the suit. Especially panty lines."

"Yeah, that was my second surprise." Sunny had pushed the bodysuit down to her feet and stepped out of it, stark naked. Kirk had kept glancing at both entrances to his little "execution chamber," kept listening for sounds of someone approaching.

"You wanted me to get dressed," Sunny said, sliding her hands up his chest.

"Well, I didn't *want* you to get dressed, I was just..."

"Inhibited."

Kirk laughed. "You were uninhibited enough for both of us."

"Part of you wasn't inhibited, though." She ran her hands over his shoulders, down his arms.

The part of him that wasn't inhibited had made his pants a tight fit. He'd tried to talk reason to her, tried to talk her into taking a ride with him to find some secluded place. Mutely she'd slid her hands up the insides of his thighs to meet in the middle. After that, all he'd managed to get out was a groan.

"Do you remember what you did next?" Kirk asked, feeling himself stir anew at the memory.

Sunny's eyes were a deep violet, the pupils wide and bottomless. "I released you."

A slow smile spread across his face. "Well, you released *part* of me." His rampant penis had sprung from his open fly into her soft, hot hands. He'd thought that was how it would end, that she'd satisfy him that way, a quick hand job. But she'd had other plans.

Kirk's voice sounded a little hoarse to his ears. "You'd never done that before. Taken me in your mouth."

Sunny smiled. "I was curious. And I wanted to please you. I didn't know how excited it would make me, kissing you there."

Kirk pulled her against himself again, letting her feel what this conversation was doing to him. "It was so incredibly erotic. Never in my life had I felt anything like that. My imagination didn't even come close. And you were so eager...and so endearingly innocent at the same time. And I couldn't even *see* you! I still had the damn hood on, and it kept me from looking down. That just made it more..." Something close to a growl escaped him. "It's a wonder I didn't shoot off like a rocket the instant I felt your lips there."

"It would've been okay if you had, but I'm glad you didn't."

"You finally got that hood off me." She'd crawled onto his lap, her knees astride him on the wide wooden chair, and worked the leather hood off. The instant his face was free, she'd kissed him, aggressively, spearing him with her tongue, hard and fast. That was something else she'd never done before, asserted herself so boldly, and it had him jerking his hips, instinctively seeking the moist core of her.

Sunny had appeared unmoved by his painfully aroused condition, by his breathless pleas. She'd quieted him by offering her breast, lifting it to his lips. Half out of his mind with lust, Kirk had latched on to it hard, suckling greedily, holding her with his teeth. The honeyed taste of her, the feel of her in his mouth, against his tongue, had inflamed him past endurance. Never had he treated her so roughly, but at the time, gentleness had been beyond him. Her shrill gasps had bounced off the partitioned walls. Just when his dazed mind had realized he might be hurting her, he'd heard her moans of encouragement. *Yes, oh yes, Kirk...*

Her hips had lowered and she'd impaled herself on him in one long, slow descent.

"As I recall," she said, "we made sparks fly."

"Literally." The instant he'd felt himself sink into her body, tighter and slipperier and hotter than any woman had a right to be, his fingers had clenched the arms of the chair, inadvertently pressing the hidden button and setting off the sparks and sizzling sounds that mimicked electrocution.

Thank God no one had come downstairs to investigate the noise, because Kirk was past worrying about an audience. If the whole party had managed to squeeze into the room, he wouldn't have noticed. He was aware of nothing except Sunny riding him, devouring him, wringing him dry.

He said, "I came so hard I thought my head was going to fly off."

"Now we're talking guillotine, not electric chair." Her hands skimmed down his sides.

Kirk kissed her, tasted her lingeringly. He plucked at her mouth as she shifted against him for greater contact. His hands slipped under the short hem of her dress, and he felt her breathing change. His fingers glided up her bare thighs to the edge of her underpants.

"You wore an old-fashioned garter belt at the wedding," he murmured against her lips. He smiled. "You still know how to surprise me."

"I'm no fan of panty hose." She breathed a sigh as his hands molded her bottom over the bikini underpants, bunching her dress around her hips.

"No garter belt now," he observed.

"Too warm for stockings. Kiss me again."

He did, and while they were linked, mouth to mouth, he turned her so her back was to the butcher block. He broke the kiss to lift her onto it. Her dress remained bunched, affording him a glimpse of her polka-dotted underpants. Sunny's eyes were drowsy with desire, her nostrils flared. Without wasting another second, Kirk grasped the zipper tab at the scoop neckline of the dress and pulled.

She was wearing a matching polka-dotted bra, cotton but with those abbreviated cups that exposed as much as they concealed.

"Front clasp," he said, undoing the hook that closed the bra. "This must be my lucky day."

"And mine," Sunny said with a lopsided smile.

The cups parted and Kirk pushed them aside. Like the rest of her figure, her breasts were a bit fuller than in high school, not quite as high as they had been, but beautiful, womanly. Perfect.

"You take my breath away." He placed a soft kiss on one puckered tip, felt it tighten further under his lips. Nothing had ever sounded as sweet as her indrawn breath. Her head dropped back; she threaded her fingers through his hair.

Kirk licked the nipple, light flicks of his tongue, goading it into a stiff knot. He sucked it into his mouth, reveling in her sharp cry, the mindless force with which she pulled him closer. At the same time he played with the other breast, shaping it in his hand, teasing the peak.

He pulled her to the edge of the butcher block and hauled her off it, wrapping her legs around his hips. Quickly he strode down the hall toward his room, locked mouth to mouth with Sunny, now squirming against him in silent entreaty.

"Da. Cup."

Ian's voice, from behind the closed door of his bedroom, froze Kirk in his tracks. His head snapped up, as did Sunny's.

"Cup! Dink!"

Sunny slid down off of Kirk. Swiftly she adjusted her clothing as he muttered a litany of swear words under his breath.

He cleared his throat. Seeing that Sunny was now decent, he opened the door to Ian's room, softly illuminated by a cartoon night-light. The toddler stood in his crib, clad in diaper and undershirt. Clutching the side rail with one hand, he rubbed a fist over one eye.

Kirk came into the room and ruffled Ian's blond curls. "What's is it, champ? I thought you were asleep."

"Dink. Firsty."

"You want a drink of water?"

"I'll get it," Sunny said from the doorway, and disappeared.

Ian yawned. Kirk lifted him out of the crib and cuddled him against his chest. As always, the feel of his son in his arms, the warmth and weight of him, the fine baby scent of his hair, triggered feelings so intense they threatened to choke him.

"You're my champ. I love you so much," Kirk whispered. "You know that, don't you?"

Ian nodded his little head, the silky curls tickling Kirk's neck. His eyelids were drooping, but he perked up when Sunny entered with a plastic sipper cup of water. He reached for it and drained half of it in one long pull.

Sunny smiled tenderly. "You really were thirsty, weren't you?" A little water dribbled out of his mouth, and she wiped his chin with her fingers. "Enough?"

Nodding, Ian let her take the cup. Kirk shifted him in his arms and lifted him over the crib rail, pretending to grunt with the effort. "You're growing so well, you're getting to be a really big boy."

That seemed to please Ian, who smiled as his father tucked him under his blanket. "Posse."

"What? Posse? I don't know what that means, Ian."

"Posse. Posse!"

The last thing Kirk wanted was for Ian to get himself worked up at this hour. Helplessly he turned to Sunny. "Any ideas?"

She stroked Ian's middle. "Parsley, sage, rosemary and thyme? Is that what you want?"

He nodded vigorously. "Posse! Sing!"

Kirk stifled a chuckle. "Do I have to stay?"

"You certainly do," Sunny said, feigning umbrage. "You can do backup vocals."

"No, thanks."

Sunny sang softly to the boy, and to Kirk's surprise, her rendition of "Scarborough Fair," the old folk song popularized by Simon and Garfunkel, was actually pleasing to the ear.

Ian nodded off again before she got to the second chorus.

Kirk said, "With any luck, he'll stay asleep this time."

Sunny glanced around the room, her gaze lingering on Ian's dresser top. Going over to it, she lifted a framed photograph and held it nearer the nightlight. Kirk's pulse picked up speed.

"She was beautiful." Sunny examined the picture of Linda and a ten-month-old Ian, taken two months before her death. Linda was cuddling her baby on the lawn of their home, both of them laughing, the breeze lifting her straight, light brown hair.

Sunny took her time looking at it before carefully replacing it on the dresser, in the precise spot it had occupied.

Kirk said, "I...I want him to know who his mother was. I want him to know how much she—" His voice cracked.

Sunny looked at him. Her eyes shone wetly in the soft light. "How much she loved him." She took his hand. "He'll never doubt that, Kirk. I just know it."

He gripped her hand hard. He took a deep breath, and one last look at Ian, sleeping peacefully. "Come on."

Quietly they left the room, leaving the door ajar.

"He really has grown so much," Kirk said. "It's hard to believe he's the same tiny thing I could practically hold in the palm of my hand."

"It won't be long before he outgrows that crib,"

she said. "He'll be demanding an honest-to-God big-boy bed before you know it."

"Getting rid of that crib will be bittersweet. A phase of his childhood gone forever."

"Well, you won't get rid of it. You'll put it in storage for the next baby."

Sunny misinterpreted the look on his face. Her expression softened; she touched his cheek. "I know you're not thinking along those lines now, Kirk. That's understandable. But you're young. Chances are, you'll remarry someday, and give Ian a brother or a sister...."

Kirk knew he'd failed to disguise his discomfort with this subject when Sunny's gentle smile faded. She dropped her hand. "I shouldn't have said anything—"

"No. You didn't..." Helplessly he shook his head. "You didn't say anything wrong, Sunny. I'm just..." He lifted her hand, brushed his lips over her knuckles. Some things had no easy answers.

She searched his eyes, her own solemn. "What are you thinking about? What's wrong?"

He couldn't look at her. All he could do was shake his head again, as if nothing were wrong, as if she'd merely imagined his despair. His gaze landed on the open door of his bedroom. But he knew it wasn't going to happen even before Sunny said, "I think I'd better get going."

His frustrated sigh said it all. Her wry expression

told him it wasn't one-sided. But now wasn't the time; the moment had been lost.

Standing on tiptoes, Sunny kissed him. "Will you tell me someday?" He hadn't fooled her.

Kirk nodded. "Someday."

5

"THIS PIECE GOES IN...uh..." Kirk squinted at the assembly instructions. "This joint here."

"No, it doesn't." Sunny made a grab for the instruction sheet, only to have him yank it out of reach. She rolled her eyes. What was it about men and do-it-yourself projects? They all seemed to think women were incapable of constructing anything more complicated than a sandwich.

They sat on Kirk's back lawn, inside an elaborate toddler play environment constructed of multicolored parachute nylon stretched over a framework of plastic tubing. Two long, roomy crawl tunnels converged at a right angle, linked by a central tentlike cube with child-size window and door openings. Kirk's parents had taken Ian to the botanical gardens today. This play tent would be a surprise for him when he returned.

If they ever got it put together.

Sunny and Kirk had just enough room inside the half-finished central cube to sit on the grass and study the instructions printed in teeny-tiny text, poorly translated from the original Swedish. Though the red, yellow and blue fabric walls of the cube were opaque, afternoon sunlight streamed through them as if they were stained glass, painting the interior, and its occupants, in watercolor tones. Kirk was shirtless in the early August heat, his only clothing a skimpy pair of black running shorts. The slightest movement caused patches of color to skate across his sun-burnished torso.

"Ian better appreciate this," he grumbled.

Sunny laughed. "Oh yeah, that'll happen. And anyway, *I'm* the one who bought this for him."

"You and your home-shopping networks. I oughta make *you* put this thing together."

"You know, for a physics professor, you seem to have a less-than-impressive grasp of matter and energy as they relate to the Fun World Deluxe Play Tunnel. Give me that pipe. It doesn't go there."

He shooed her hands away from the plastic tube he was attempting to jam into a too-small joint. "This thing is defective."

"Uh-huh. It couldn't be that this piece goes here—" she pointed to a different joint "—and this other, *smaller* tube, the tube that looks like it's made just for this spot, goes here. Could it?" She slipped it neatly into place.

Kirk frowned at her handiwork, then stuck his nose back in the instruction sheet. Sunny ripped the paper out of his hand, wadded it up and tossed it out the porthole that passed for a window.

"Sometimes you have to figure things out by doing," she said. "Not all answers can be found in the written word, Professor."

"Why, how immensely profound. How's an eighteen-month-old supposed to negotiate this thing, anyway? It's like some giant hamster habitat. My first apartment wasn't this big."

"He'll love it. Don't you wish you'd had something like this when you were a kid?"

"In my day we played in cardboard boxes and were happy to have them."

"Well, old-timer, welcome to the twenty-first century. Here. Hold this." In a few swift moves, Sunny finished putting together the cube. "Ta-daaa!"

Kirk was wide-eyed. "How'd you do that?"

"Didn't you ever play with Tinker Toys? Oh, that's right. All you had was cardboard boxes. Gosh, I think I'm going to cry."

"My, aren't we smug." Kirk rested his forearm on a raised knee. "I may be lousy at putting together human hamster habitats, but I have my talents."

"You do, huh?" He probably hadn't meant it to sound suggestive, but for the last week and a half since they'd almost made love, Sunny had been in a near constant state of frustration. The few times she and Kirk had been able to see each other had been in the company of others: taking Ian to the zoo, attending one of the spectacular parties Amanda loved to throw, and taking in the latest Spielberg movie with Charli and Grant, who'd just returned from their three-week honeymoon trip to Italy and Greece.

Then again, judging by the way Kirk was looking at her, maybe she wasn't the only one who'd been frustrated.

"What?" he asked, with a secret little smile. "You don't think I'm a talented guy?"

"Well, I know you *used* to have your talents, way back in high school. But I mean, it's been a long time, right? Maybe the years have taken their toll." She added pointedly, "Old-timer."

The corners of Kirk's eyes crinkled. "I know a challenge when I hear one."

Sunny's heartbeat skittered. "I don't know..." she said sadly. "A guy who can't even put together a simple play tent?"

He reached for her, and she neatly evaded him, scooting to the edge of the cube. His smile turned feral, reminding Sunny that he could strike like a cobra when he chose to.

Without wasting another second, she dove into the nearest crawl tunnel, which glowed with the same sun-washed colors as the cube. Laughing, she scampered toward the patch of grass visible at the end. She'd nearly made it when Kirk's bare feet appeared in the round opening, and then his grinning face as he bent down to taunt her.

"You can run, but you can't hide!" he crowed.

She jerked to a stop. "No fair! I can't get up any speed in this dress." Her short, India-print sundress tangled under her knees as she crawled.

"So take it off."

"Now, how did I know that would be your solution?" As she spoke, she backed up swiftly. There was no room in the tunnel to turn around. Just as her butt approached the entrance to the cube, two big hands grabbed it and pulled. But Sunny was prepared for this move. She released the shoulder ties of her dress and scampered forward again, leaving Kirk holding a handful of gauzy fabric. The tunnel reverberated with her giddy laughter.

Halfway to the end, clad only in bra and panties, she peered over her shoulder, to see Kirk peering back from the cube.

"This is quite a view," he said, eyeing her raised derriere appreciatively. "I hope my neighbor, old Reverend Hargity, isn't peeking over the fence when you make a run for the house like that."

"Who said I'll be running? Maybe I'll stroll over and have a nice chat with the rev."

Kirk's rich chuckle said he wouldn't put it past her. She watched him crawl out of the cube via the small oval doorway. Soon the tunnel was shifting. Kirk was dragging it by the end.

"Did you know you can connect the two tunnels with these nifty Velcro tabs?" he asked conversationally.

No, actually, she hadn't known that.

He added, "Something I learned from that instruction sheet you never glanced at."

Sure enough, when Sunny cautiously crawled through the now curved tunnel toward what should have been the opening, she saw that it had been linked to the other tunnel to form one long loop. The cube was now the sole entrance and exit.

"Trapped!" A laugh infected Sunny's voice as sensual anticipation surged. "Like a rat!"

"That'll teach you to mess with a physicist."

She heard him crawl back into the cube. Stifling a nervous giggle, she listened intently, trying to discern which branch of the tunnel Kirk would take to get to her, certain that he had no intention of waiting her out. She had a tactical advantage, though, being closer in size to the tykes this contraption was created for.

The instant she heard him squeeze into the section of tunnel behind her, she scrabbled forward with all due haste. So intent was she on her goal that she failed to anticipate the classic fake-out. As the interior of the cube came into view, Kirk's arm abruptly appeared in the opening, snaking out to seize her wrist.

She yelped and tried to wriggle backward. With a wicked cackle he captured her other wrist and hauled her out of the tunnel onto the square of grass inside the cube. In a flash he rolled on top of her, one-handedly shackling her wrists above her head. His breathless laughter echoed hers. A little thrill swept her as she realized that this time, she wasn't going to get away.

The grass felt cool and prickly beneath her, in contrast to the welcome weight and heat of Kirk on top of her. Both of them were nearly naked, and the feel of skin on skin went to her head like potent wine. Sunlight suffused the colorful walls of their haven, casting rainbow hues everywhere. It was like being inside a kaleidoscope.

Kirk leaned up on an elbow and looked at her. Whatever he saw turned his pale blue eyes to smoky slate. One long, hair-dusted leg pressed between hers as he lowered his head and kissed her. Sunny felt her body rise as she gave herself up to the kiss, felt her free leg slide up to hook over his. At that moment, she needed Kirk more than she needed air.

He released her hands to unfasten her bra and toss it aside, before throwing himself into the kiss once more. His hot, thrusting tongue, the insistent ridge of his erection between them, spiked her excitement to new heights. When he relinquished her mouth, it was to press kisses to her throat, her chest, and lower, to her aching breasts, sensitized beyond belief. She emitted desperate little sounds as he stroked and nipped and sucked her, first gently, then with increasing force, until she was writhing against him, clawing his shoulders.

He pulled back, his eyes darker than she'd ever seen them, his lips moist, his color high.

"I can't wait," Sunny gasped, shameless in her need. She felt as if she'd been waiting twelve years for this very moment. "Please, Kirk, I can't wait any longer."

He stripped off her panties with breathtaking

speed. His running shorts followed, and suddenly he was inside her, high, hard and deep. Sunny bit her lip against the scream of pleasure that barreled up her throat.

She wrapped her legs around him as he tilted her hips, fitting themselves to each other as if they'd never been apart. The feel of Kirk moving inside her, filling her with long, sure strokes, plumbing the deepest heart of her, obliterated the last vestige of Sunny's self-control. Raw instinct took over as she met his pistoning thrusts, clung to him, reaching, reaching....

Kirk watched her, his eyes like banked coals, glowing with a hot blue light. Cords stood out in his neck. He leaned more heavily into her, angling her lower body for greater contact, nudging the tiny bud of her desire with every fierce lunge. Sunny's mouth opened on a silent scream. The tension in her body peaked as he held her on the enchanted brink of orgasm for one long, heart-stopping moment.

Just when Sunny thought her mind would shatter from the pure, stunning pleasure of anticipation, her climax wrapped its long fingers around her and squeezed. Her back bowed sharply as she tumbled over the edge. Kirk plunged into her straining body, fast and rough, his eyes half-closed, his features tortured.

Holding her in a steel grip, he rammed hard into her, groaning deep in his throat. She felt the potent intensity of his release, felt the pulsing salvo at the depths of her womb.

They collapsed in a sweaty heap, gulping air. Sunny felt as if she were drifting outside herself. She squinted at the sunlight streaming through the bright-hued walls of the cube, savored the sweet aftershocks that told her how deeply she and Kirk were still joined. She felt a little raw where the grass had scraped the skin of her back, but she didn't mind. Kirk was here, her Viking, her golden lover, and that was all that mattered.

He raised his head and grinned down at her. Sunny couldn't have said who started laughing first, or what they were laughing at. Not that the absurdity of the setting wasn't reason enough. She just knew it felt as if her life had only now begun, as if she'd just awoken from a twelve-year hibernation.

Kirk kissed her and rolled off of her, cradling her against his steady heartbeat. Eventually he asked, "Is it like you remember?"

She smiled. "Better." Kirk had been eager and inventive as a teenager, and devoted to her—everything a young girl could hope for. But the boy he'd been then couldn't hold a candle to the mature man she now found herself with.

"Ditto," he murmured, nuzzling her hair.

"We were in a pretty big hurry just now."

His amused grunt said, *No kidding.*

"And careless," she added.

"Huh?"

Men! Sunny leaned up to look at him, chuckling at his perplexed expression. "I'm talking about protection, Professor. You know, birth control?"

Kirk went utterly still, his expression as sober as she'd ever seen it. He looked like he wanted to say something, but instead he tucked her against his chest once more. His heartbeat was faster now, agitated. Perhaps he'd assumed she was on the Pill or something. If so, it was a hell of an assumption.

"Look," she said, "I don't really think we have anything to worry about. It's not my, you know, fertile time right now." He said nothing. "Okay?"

She felt him swallow thickly. "Okay."

"So...do you want to take care of it?"

"Take care of...? Oh, buying condoms. Yeah. Of course," he said dully. "You shouldn't have to do that."

Sunny smiled against his chest, already fantasizing about some future time when she and Kirk would once again make love without birth control—by design rather than accident.

6

"AH, THE LADIES of leisure have arrived!" Amanda Coppersmith announced.

Standing with Raven and Charli in the doorway of their friend's office, Sunny watched a grinning Amanda lean back in her burgundy leather executive chair and toss her Mont Blanc fountain pen onto the pile of papers before her. When the dark-haired man seated in front of Amanda's glass-topped desk turned toward the doorway, Sunny recognized Brent Radley, Raven's brother-in-law and the sales manager of *Grasshopper*, the children's magazine Amanda published. Brent's handsome features stretched into a welcoming smile.

"Ladies of leisure indeed," he said, smirking at the many shopping bags they toted, printed with the logos of Saks Fifth Avenue, Bloomingdale's and Lord & Taylor.

Sunny strolled into the office. "For your information, I'm off today. I'll be slaving away tomorrow and Sunday, though, while you get the whole weekend off, you lazy bum."

Raven shoved her chin-length, dark blond hair behind her ear. "And both my hypnotherapy clients for today canceled their appointments. So there."

"And school doesn't even *start* until next week!" Charli put in. "So *double* there!"

"So be forewarned," Sunny said. "One more 'ladies of leisure' crack and you'll be wearing this." She wagged a hefty brown take-out sack.

Amanda straightened. "What've you got there? Smells like..." She sniffed the air. "Greek!"

"Good nose," Raven said. "Gyros, spinach pie, souvlaki, and a little Middle Eastern thrown in."

Charli said, "We figured we'd just spread it out in the conference room and share."

"Looks like you exercised some restraint, Raven." Brent eyed the one tiny shopping bag his sister-in-law and onetime girlfriend had set in a corner. "Good news for my brother."

"Yeah, well, don't be impressed yet." Raven nodded toward the heap of bags Charli and Sunny were piling next to it. "They wouldn't let me carry my own stuff. I'm just three months along. The way they fussed over me, you'd think I was about to give birth right there in the shoe department."

"Trust you to complain about being fussed over," Amanda said, rising and coming around her desk to inspect the purchases. As always, she was elegantly attired, her pale blond hair pulled back into a sleek chignon. Her short-skirted suit in vivid raspberry showed off her willowy figure and long, slim legs. "Hey, if it were me with a bun in the oven, you can bet your baby bootees I'd milk it for all it was worth."

"If it were you with a bun in the oven," Charli said, "I'd die of shock."

Amanda had sworn off marriage the day her second divorce became final last year. Nevertheless, she was scheduled to become the fourth and final beneficiary of the Wedding Ring matchmaking pact when her thirtieth birthday rolled around on October 7, a mere six weeks away. Just how Sunny and the others would persuade her to cooperate had yet to be determined.

Amanda hadn't always had an aversion to marriage—after all, she'd given it the old college try not once but twice! Even now, Sunny wondered how much of her friend's reticence was actually a selfprotective impulse, a subconscious attempt to spare herself more pain.

"My, my," Amanda said, pulling a pair of maternity leggings out of one of the shopping bags. She held them up, stretching the roomy elastic panel. "Aren't these fetching."

Brent looked dubious. "You aren't going to get that big." He eyed Raven's midriff, just beginning to expand; his blue eyes widened. "Are you?"

Raven laughed. "It's not a permanent condition. After the baby comes, I'll pass these things on to..." She waggled her eyebrows at Charli, who blushed to the roots of her dark brown hair.

"We're—we're not—" Charli stammered. "What makes you think—"

"We all see the way you and your gorgeous bridegroom look at each other," Amanda said, now rummaging through one of Sunny's bags from Lord & Taylor. "Don't tell me you guys aren't even *trying*. Will you look at this. Someone's going to be the belle of the beach." She held up a two-piece swimsuit, royal blue with silver trim. Inspecting the tag, she added, "Sunny's size. Half price! Good work, girl!"

"Why don't you model it for us?" Brent suggested.

"Yeah, that'll happen," Sunny muttered.

Raven smirked at her brother-in-law. "Might I remind you, Mr. Radley, that you're married to a *swimsuit model*? As in a woman who is so drop-dead gorgeous she is *paid* to prance around in little triangles of cloth that make Sunny's new bathing suit look like it was designed by Omar the Tentmaker."

"Gee, thanks," Sunny said.

"So?" Brent said.

"*So*," Raven continued, "what woman—what *normal-looking* woman—in her right mind would willingly model a swimsuit for you, knowing what you go home to at night?"

"Oh, you can't be serious." Brent spread his hands. "You're all lovely women. And anyway, don't you know variety is the spice of life?"

Sunny bit her lip and avoided looking at the others, knowing she'd never be able to keep a straight face if she did. Until recently, variety had been very much the spice of Brent's life, sexually speaking—until Marina, the swimsuit model, had come along. A canny lady who knew what—and who—she wanted, Marina had patiently waited out his doomed relationship with Raven and then put her roving man on a short leash. To Sunny's knowledge, he hadn't strayed since, and the two of them had been happily married since April.

Amanda looked toward the open doorway. "Were your ears burning?"

Sunny turned to see who her friend was addressing. If possible, Marina Radley was even more astonishingly beautiful than the last time Sunny had seen her. The olive-skinned young woman stood several inches taller than Amanda, who was a good five-seven. Marina's hip-length black hair and almond-shaped eyes gave her an exotic appeal that had served her well in the cutthroat world of modeling. But no one had to tell Marina that looks fade in time. Anticipating the inevitable, she'd begun pursuing a career in holistic medicine.

Brent came to his feet and kissed his wife. Marina greeted everyone and gave Raven a warm hug. Despite the fact that Marina had once been "the other woman," she and Raven were now family, having married brothers, and in fact had become quite close over the past months.

"Stay and have lunch with us," Raven said. "It's

Greek, so it's partly veggie." Marina was a confirmed vegetarian.

"Oh, thanks, but we have reservations at Sue Ann's," Marina said, naming a hot new health-food eatery.

Brent's shoulders slumped. "I haven't had souvlaki in I don't know how long," he whined.

"Sue Ann makes an outrageous grilled-veggie sandwich. Your conscience—and your arteries—will thank me." Marina slipped her arm through his and firmly ushered him out of the office. "Enjoy your lunch," she called by way of farewell, as her husband gazed longingly at the grease-stained take-out bag.

Within two minutes the Wedding Ring pals had arranged their feast on the sprawling, glossy table in the conference room. Closing the door for privacy, Amanda took her seat. "Dibs on the spinach pie."

"Down, girl." Sunny was busy prying lids off foil containers and unwrapping warm grilled pita bread. "There's plenty to go around. Help me get this stuff open."

Charli handed out paper plates and napkins while Raven opened a bottle of diet soda. "Is Kirk all ready for the start of classes?" Raven asked Sunny.

"Yep." Sunny scooped some hummus, a garlicky chick-pea dip, onto her plate and tore a piece of flat pita bread. "He'll be teaching introductory physics and a couple of more advanced courses. He's looking forward to it."

Raven said, "So things are still good between you two?"

Sunny couldn't restrain a grin. "They seem to be. We've really, I don't know, meshed. If anything, it's better than it was in high school."

Raven squeezed Sunny's hand. "I'm happy for you."

Amanda reached past Charli for the falafel, fried balls of seasoned, ground chick peas. "What about the sex? Is *that* better than in the old days?"

"Amanda!" Raven barked.

Sunny chuckled. "Kirk asked the same thing. The first time. I have no complaints. Let's leave it at that."

"Say it." Amanda forked up a bite of savory spinach pie, with its golden-brown striations of papery phyllo dough.

"Say what?" Sunny asked.

"Say, 'You were right and I was wrong.'"

"About me and Kirk?"

Charli said, "You were pretty opposed to the idea at the beginning, as I recall."

Sunny rolled her eyes, but she was still smiling. "I thought you guys were nuts."

"Sometimes," Raven said with a tender smile of her own, "your friends really do know what's best for you."

"That was the idea behind this whole pact, wasn't it?" Charli poured herself some soda. "I mean, we've known each other since kindergarten. Who better to choose our husbands?"

"Anyone want to split a gyro?" Amanda asked, pulling the sandwich of pita and spicy pressed lamb closer.

Charli said, "I will. I fell so in love with Greek food on our honeymoon, I must've gained five pounds. I'm afraid to get on the scale."

"Don't worry about it." Amanda sawed the sandwich in half with a plastic knife and handed Charli her portion. "You'll be preggers soon enough if you aren't already, and then you'll be in those big, ugly leggings with the elastic panels."

Raven gave Amanda an exasperated scowl.

"So back to Sunny and her high-school sweetheart," Amanda said. "You've been together how long now?"

"Seven weeks."

"Has he told you he—" Amanda batted her eyelashes "—*loves* you yet?"

Raven said, "That's none of your business, Amanda. Sunny, don't answer that."

"I don't mind." Sunny pushed her food around on her plate. "He hasn't actually said he loves me." She looked at each of her friends in turn. "But I know he does. I mean, I just *know* it."

Raven said gently, "What do you think he's waiting for?"

Sunny took a deep breath. "I'm not really sure. Sometimes I get the feeling that something's troubling him."

Charli drizzled yogurt sauce on her gyro. "Have you asked him about it?"

"Once or twice." Sunny shrugged. "Whatever it is, he doesn't want to talk about it."

"He *did* just lose his wife," Amanda pointed out. "Maybe that's it."

"That was, what?" Charli said. "Eight months ago?"

"Just about," Sunny said.

A small frown appeared on Amanda's brow. "He could still be grieving. That kind of trauma...it takes a long time to get over it."

The other three fell silent. This didn't sound like their brash friend. But on reflection, Sunny realized Amanda was no stranger to trauma herself, having endured two rancorous divorces in the space of three years. Not on a par with the death of a spouse, perhaps, but Sunny knew the experience had left its mark on Amanda. She'd always been mouthy, with a sarcastic wit not everyone appreciated, but lately she'd displayed a deep cynicism toward life that saddened her closest friends.

"Well, that could be it, Linda's death," Sunny said, "but I don't think so. I mean, he still misses her, of course. He's still getting over it—that's only natural. But I really don't think that's the problem."

Charlie said, "You love him, don't you?"

Sunny gave her a wry smile. "You have to ask?"

"Then you should tell him. Why wait for him to make the first move?"

Sunny caught the smile that Raven and Amanda exchanged. Before she'd met Grant, shy, mousy Charli Rossi would never have accepted such bold advice herself—much less offered it.

"Things will happen at their own pace," Sunny said. "I'm in no hurry."

Her friends greeted this statement with shrill laughter and hoots of derision. Amanda said, "Honey, you've been in a hurry to get married since you were eighteen."

"All right, all right." Sunny's pals knew her too well. "What I mean is, if it takes Kirk a little longer to...feel comfortable with all this, for whatever reason, then I can wait."

"As long as you don't have to wait *too* long," Charli said with a naughty smile.

"That's right." Amanda blotted her mouth with a napkin. "There's that old biological clock ticking away."

"Don't listen to her," Raven said. "Thirty-year-old women have plenty of time left on their biological clocks. Look at me. It took no time at all for me to get pregnant."

Sunny knew she had the sappiest grin on her face, but she didn't care. "It's just so hard to believe that after all this time, my dream is finally taking shape." She shook her head in wonder. "By this time next year, it could be *me* wearing those ugly maternity leggings! Pass me some of that gyro!"

7

SUNNY MUMBLED, "Are you hungry?" Lying in Kirk's arms amid her disheveled bedcovers, she felt his chuckle as a rumbling vibration deep in his chest.

"That's a joke, right? I'm ravenous!"

He'd arrived at Sunny's apartment around six o'clock for dinner. It was now nearly eight and the swordfish steaks sat untouched in the refrigerator, steeping in a piquant lime-ginger marinade. The table was half-set, the salad half-made, and Sunny was one-hundred-percent satisfied.

"Well, it's not my fault dinner never got on the table." She stretched luxuriously. "*Someone* distracted me."

Kirk's singular brand of distraction had left a trail of clothing from the kitchen to Sunny's bedroom, which was decorated in shades of rose, cream and sage green. The sky outside the lace-draped, fourth-story window was not yet fully dark on this balmy late August evening.

Kirk's stomach squealed, prompting Sunny to give it a playful smack. "Tell you what," he offered. "You get that fish going and I'll finish throwing together the salad. Salad I can do."

"You got yourself a deal." As Sunny flicked on the bedside lamp, her gaze lit on the torn condom packet resting on her nightstand. "Oh, I meant to tell you. I made an appointment with my doctor. I'm going on the Pill." Swinging her feet off the bed, she lifted her pink-and-white seersucker robe off the rocking chair and slipped her arms into it. When Kirk didn't respond, she turned to face him. He was sitting up now, partially covered by the floral-printed sheet, his expression grim.

"Now, don't argue." She tied the robe's sash. "I know you don't like using condoms, and the Pill is more reliable. Plus it's much safer than it was in the old days—the dosage is a lot lower."

He stared at the cluster of family photos on the opposite wall, but something about his inward-directed gaze told Sunny he wasn't seeing them. A shiver crawled up her spine. Slowly she sat on the edge of the bed.

Kirk opened his mouth to speak, and closed it. Finally he turned bleak eyes to her. "I can't let you do that."

Sunny swallowed around a hard lump of foreboding. "Go on the Pill? Why not?"

"I probably should've told you sooner. Instead of letting you keep on thinking..."

Sunny followed his gaze to the condom packet. "Kirk, whatever it is, it can't be that—"

"I've had a vasectomy."

His words kicked her in the solar plexus. "What?"

"Eleven months after Ian was born. Linda and I decided one child was enough. How could I have known..."

That one month later, Linda would be dead.

He stated the obvious. "I can't father any more children."

Sunny's pulse drummed hard in her throat. Like a robot she turned to stare at the square packet on her nightstand, with one end ripped off. Her voice was a rasp. "You...you deceived me."

"Sunny, I love you."

She pressed on her temples, as if to block out those three words she'd waited weeks to hear.

"Please listen to me," he said. "I had my reasons—"

He touched her arm and she jerked away, coming unsteadily to her feet. "What reasons can excuse something like this?" Stinging tears stood in her eyes.

"You mean so much to me." His tortured gaze pleaded for understanding. "I knew very early—as soon as we started seeing each other—that we belonged together."

"That's why you—you lied to me?"

No matter what he said, it *was* a lie! True, he'd never claimed that he could get her pregnant, but he'd actively fostered her assumption that he could. The empty condom packet was damningly eloquent.

He looked her in the eye. "Do you love me?"

"Don't." She raised her hands as if to ward off a blow.

"Answer me, Sunny. Do you love me?"

"I—I thought I did. Now..." Pressing her fingers to her mouth, she choked back a sob. "Damn you, Kirk. Yes, I loved you. I *trusted* you!"

His eyes briefly squeezed shut.

"That's what love means," she cried. "It's what it's *supposed* to mean. Trust! I never thought you'd trick me like this—"

"I didn't trick you."

"What do you call it?" She tossed the empty condom packet at him. "You let me believe in us. In a future! You let me *dream!*"

"Don't you see? That's why I couldn't tell you. I know about your dream. I know how badly you want children." He rose from the bed.

She backed away.

"I love your dream," he said quietly. "It's part of you. If I could give you those children you want so much, if I could make your dream come true...oh, my love, I'd do it in a heartbeat. I'd have proposed to you already if—"

"If you weren't so busy manipulating me."

Kirk's features hardened. "Let me ask you this. Back in early July, when we first met up again. If you'd known this about me, that I couldn't give you children, would you have gotten involved with me? Would you have let yourself fall in love with me?"

Sunny's mouth worked soundlessly for a moment.

Would she have? "It should've been my decision to make. You shouldn't have taken that choice away from me."

"Perhaps you're right. I did it because I need you." He spread his arms, laying open his soul. "I need you, Sunny. I need you in my life. I thought maybe, by the time you found out about this, you'd feel the same way about me and it would...it would work out. We'd make it work out."

She hugged herself. "You were trying to...to give yourself an edge. An unfair advantage."

"What would you have done in my place?"

"I wouldn't have betrayed your trust."

"I never meant to hurt you. Please believe that."

Sunny dragged in a shaky breath. "I want you to leave now, Kirk."

After a moment he said, "We need to talk about this some more."

"Not now. I...I can't."

"Not now, but we will deal with this. I'm not giving you up, Sunny."

Holding her robe closed, she said, "I can't sleep with you anymore." She made herself meet his desolate gaze. "I can't share myself with you...that way...if we have no future together."

A muscle jumped in his cheek. "You're telling me we're through."

Sunny clutched her robe so tightly her fingers ached. She wanted to tell him yes, they were through. She wanted to hurt Kirk as deeply as he'd hurt her. But did she want it badly enough to let him walk out of her life for good?

The fact was, that was another decision that had been taken away from her. She'd vowed to abide by the rules of the Wedding Ring pact, which required her to give the relationship three full months unless Kirk called it quits before then. That meant five more weeks.

Her chin trembled as she said, "No. No, that's not what I'm saying. Not yet."

Kirk's shoulders visibly relaxed. "Well. I guess that's something." Snatching his briefs off the carpet, he stepped into them and reached for his jeans. "I'll leave now, Sunny. In a few days, when you've had some time to think about this, about why I...why I deceived you, we'll talk again."

8

"WHADDAYA THINK, Ian?" Grant Sterling asked. "Are we building it right?"

The toddler, squatting on a small rug on the other side of the half-finished basement, looked up from his Fisher-Price workbench and the plastic nail he was vigorously pounding into it with his play hammer. Gravely he contemplated the newly erected two-by-four framework. He nodded. "Uh-huh."

"Whew." Hunter Radley paused in the act of measuring a length of wallboard, to grin at Kirk. "I was worried we'd have to tear it down and start over."

The basement windows were all open, but the early September day was hot and the three men had already stripped off their shirts, prompting little Ian to do the same. He worked on his side of the room, clad in sandals and a pair of red shorts thickly padded by his diaper.

Kirk secured the last two-by-four in place with an electric screw gun. "You need another juice box, son?"

"Uh-uh."

"You can come over and take a look now."

Kirk had been tempted to let his parents watch Ian

while he, with Grant's and Hunter's help, constructed a new wall in the basement, to divide it into two distinct spaces: a utility room for the washer, dryer and furnace, and a separate playroom for his son. Ian, however, fascinated by the prospect of a wall where there was only open space, had wanted to stay and "help."

Kirk had capitulated, on the condition that the toddler keep his distance when power tools were in use. He'd been especially careful when installing the wooden soleplate with the rented nail gun, which used .22-caliber cartridges to drive long nails into the concrete floor. While Kirk and Hunter had used that thing, Grant had held the squirming boy in his arms, well away from the action.

Kirk now lifted Ian and let him inspect the framework, explaining how the wallboard would soon be attached to it. "I help!" Ian insisted, even as he rubbed his eyes.

"Of course," Kirk said. "I really need your help. But first let's get you into a dry diaper, okay?" Ian nodded sleepily.

As he carried his son upstairs, Kirk glanced at his buddies over his shoulder and mouthed "nap." Five minutes later Ian was softly snoring in his crib. Kirk switched on the nursery monitor and brought the receiver down to the basement, along with three frosty bottles of beer. Hunter and Grant were engaged in some good-natured bickering over how many times it was necessary to measure the wallboard before it was cut.

"You must've heard the saying," Hunter mumbled around the pencil he held clamped between his teeth as he measured a length of wallboard to accommodate the low dropped ceiling. Wearing a twisted red bandanna as a sweatband around his dark, collar-length hair, and with his bare upper body deeply suntanned, he almost looked like a Native American.

"What saying?"

"Measure twice, cut once."

Grant accepted a bottle of beer. "Sounds like the voice of bitter experience. I thought you lived in an apartment until you married Raven."

Carefully Hunter marked the wallboard. "The building housing Stitches has been around for eighty-something years," he said, referring to his two-year-old comedy club. "I'm still struggling to make a living. If I went and hired a handyman every time the roof leaked or some floor tiles needed to be replaced, I'd never make it out of the red. Hand me the utility knife, would ya?"

"How do you change the blade on this damn thing?"

Kirk watched Grant struggle with the knife for a few moments before relieving him of the chore. "Wasn't your old man a construction worker?" he asked as he replaced the pitted blade with a fresh one.

"Yeah." Grant shrugged. "So?"

"So you don't know a socket wrench from a screw-driver. Didn't you learn anything at your daddy's knee?"

"Sure. I learned how to stay out of the bastard's way. It was the only lesson that really sunk in."

Kirk exchanged a meaningful glance with Hunter as he handed him the knife. Sunny had told Kirk that Grant had endured an abusive upbringing before running away from home at sixteen, but until Grant had shed his shirt and Kirk had gotten a look at the scars crisscrossing his back, he hadn't realized just how bad it had been.

Kirk figured it was time to change the subject, but Hunter beat him to it. "So, Kirk. What did you *really* think about that show last night?" His conspiratorial smile said, *Now that the women aren't around to hear*.

"A little too politically correct for my tastes."

"What show?" Grant asked.

Hunter said, "The four of us went to the city to see a new off-Broadway musical about sexual discrimination in the workplace."

Grant's eyebrows lifted. "A *musical?*"

"A musical," Kirk confirmed, as he hauled the trimmed piece of plasterboard to the framed-in wall. "Number twenty-six on my top-ten list of favorite entertainments." He held the board in place while Hunter affixed it with the screw gun. "This particular musical had a song called 'Tell It to the EEOC.'"

Hunter said, "And who can forget that crowd-pleaser 'Glass Ceiling Boogie-woogie.'"

"Catchy," Grant agreed. He ran his hand over the screw heads dimpling the edges of the wallboard. "We slap joint compound over these, right? After the drywall is all up?"

"You're learning." Hunter stood back to examine his handiwork. "Then tape, then more mud."

"Mud?"

"Joint compound." Kirk stretched his arms back and felt something pop. He rotated his shoulders, working out the kinks. "It'll take several coats. It has to dry and be sanded between coats."

"Then we're done?" Grant asked.

"Then we prime and paint," Hunter said.

"Fire-engine red," Kirk said. The other two looked at him. "I believe in letting kids make decisions. And anyway, it's a playroom, right?"

"Hey, why not?" Hunter said. "Back in college, I painted my dorm room all black." He started humming "Glass Ceiling Boogie-woogie," until Kirk aimed the screw gun at him menacingly.

"Next time we double-date," Hunter said, "you and I get to pick the place."

"I vote for the demolition derby," Kirk said.

"Now you're talking."

"You'd have been spared that torture last night if things were normal between Sunny and me."

Kirk could tell by the looks on his pals' faces that they'd heard about his troubles with Sunny. Three days had passed since she'd found out about his vasectomy. She must have confided in her friends, and they in turn had told their husbands.

He added, "She refuses to see me alone. It has to be with another couple. I don't know how we're supposed to talk and make things right if we can't even have a little privacy."

Hunter said, "Sunny did seem kind of aloof last night. Maybe she just needs a little time to, you know, adjust."

"At least she hasn't broken up with me," Kirk said. "Not officially, anyway."

A heavy silence descended as Grant and Hunter applied themselves to the task of measuring the wallboard. Kirk had the uneasy feeling they knew something he didn't. But that was ridiculous. What insights could they possibly have about him and Sunny?

"Why don't you cut it this time?" Hunter asked Grant.

"You mean you trust me with this thing?" Grant accepted the utility knife with a wry smile. Using the yardstick, he did a creditable job of cutting through the drywall, then splitting the paper backing. He carried it to the framework and held it while Kirk screwed it in place.

Kirk said, "Sunny wouldn't even come in the house to say hi to Ian when the three of you picked me up last night. Did you notice?"

"Yeah," Hunter said. "I noticed."

"I know why she stayed in the car." Kirk squatted

to place the last few screws. "She doesn't want him getting too close to her. Which tells me—" he stood "—that she knows our relationship is doomed. I guess I should be grateful, right?" he added bitterly. "She has my son's welfare at heart."

"They really get along, don't they?" Grant asked. "Sunny and Ian."

Kirk nodded. "They hit it off right from the start. Sunny's a natural with kids. She's got this strong maternal—" His voice cracked. Hunter and Grant pretended they hadn't noticed.

"I let her down," Kirk said simply.

"Don't be so hard on yourself." Hunter leaned against the newel post at the foot of the stairway. Yanking the bandanna off his head, he wiped his sweat-sheened chest with it.

"Sunny has...well, not to put too overdramatic a spin on it, but she's given me back my joy in life," Kirk said. "She's given me her love, unreservedly. And I've repaid her with nothing but misery. The one thing she wants most in the world, I can't give her."

Grant said, "Kirk, no one has a crystal ball. Listen, I've known you only for a couple of months, but that's long enough to know you're not impulsive, or irresponsible. I figure you and Linda thought long and hard about that vasectomy before you did it." He spread his hands. "How could you have known how things would turn out? Stop beating yourself up over it."

Kirk sank down on the bottom steps, setting his beer bottle next to him. "I want to marry Sunny. There's practically no chance of that now."

"Can't vasectomies be surgically reversed?" Grant asked.

"The doctor who did mine talked about that, but to tell you the truth, I didn't pay much attention. At the time, I was thinking of sterility as a permanent step. I do know he said reversals don't always work."

Hunter shoved his bandanna in his jeans pocket. "But isn't it worth looking into?"

"When it's obvious that Sunny's already given up on us? What am I supposed to tell her? That there's a chance I can undo the vasectomy? A chance I'll be able to father more children? What if I go through with the operation and it doesn't work? No, for me to even consider a major step like that, I'd have to know she was behind me a hundred percent. And that's just not the case." Kirk picked at the label on his beer bottle. "God, just when my life seemed to be turning around...just when I was starting to feel like I had a little control over it..."

Grant's grim smile was eloquent. "Believe me, admitting how little control you really have beats the hell out of a false sense of confidence."

Hunter turned to Grant. "If you're worried that you're getting overconfident, get your wife pregnant. That's one big, bad reality check, my friend."

"Amen." Kirk lifted his beer bottle and clinked it against Hunter's.

Grant's smile turned into a full-fledged grin. "Well, uh, that's one reality check that may come sooner rather than later."

His pals hooted. "I knew it!" Kirk said.

"She's not pregnant yet," Grant hastened to add.

"Then you'll have to apply yourself a little more diligently," Hunter said with a smirk. "Stop working late so many nights. Stop trying so hard to make partner."

"Charli would kill me if she knew I'd spilled the beans," Grant fretted. "She wants to keep it private till it's a done deal. Don't tell Raven and Sunny!"

His friends laughed.

"I'm serious!"

"All right, all right," Kirk said. "We never heard a thing."

"This is a hundred and eighty degrees from the kind of marriage I thought I'd have," Grant said with a little smile, "the kind of marriage I carefully orchestrated for the sake of my career."

"You must've wanted to make partner pretty bad," Hunter said. Grant's obsessive desire to become a partner in his stuffy Wall Street law firm had been the driving force behind his original decision to marry Charli.

"Things have changed," Grant said. "My priorities have been completely turned around. I'd still like to make partner, but it's not the most important thing in my life anymore."

Charli was. He didn't have to say it.

"We weren't going to have children," Grant continued. "Well, *I* wasn't going to have children, and by the time Charli found out there'd be no kids, and no sex, it was our wedding night—too late for her to back out."

Kirk frowned. "You waited till you were married before telling her?"

"No, I thought she understood beforehand. It was a mix-up. My fault. I knew she was getting a raw deal, but for the longest time I stuck to my guns, stubborn son of a bitch that I am—denying my feelings and rejecting her love." With a self-deprecating smile he told Kirk, "So take it from me, there are worse things than knowing that some things are out of your control."

"But even when Charli thought she'd never have children with you," Kirk said, "she stuck it out. To Sunny, having a family is everything. As much as you wanted to make partner—that's how she feels about marrying the right guy and raising a houseful of kids. It's all she's ever wanted."

Hunter spoke up. "But you and Sunny already have Ian. I thought you said she was close to him."

"She adores Ian. And he adores her. But it's not the same as having her own."

"There's always adoption."

"I don't think she'd consider it," Kirk said miserably. "It's not part of her plan, what she's been waiting her whole life for."

"I don't know," Grant said. "If it turns out I'm shooting blanks or something—if I can't give Charli children—I'll feel lousy, of course, but speaking as a matrimonial lawyer, I've gotta tell you, it's the husband and wife who form the foundation of a family. The strength of their union, their teamwork, will make or break it. Just look at all those couples who stay together 'for the sake of the children.' Everyone ends up miserable when there's no underlying structure to support the family. It's like putting up drywall without this." He slapped the wooden framework of the wall they were building.

"I've gotta agree," Hunter said. "Get the right two people together and you can overcome almost any obstacle."

"I *thought* Sunny was the right one for me. But I have a feeling this is one obstacle that can't be overcome." Kirk glanced at Hunter. "You're right, she was aloof last night. Like it was some kind of chore just spending time in my company. I don't know why she's still seeing me." He sighed raggedly. "I'm going to let her go—pull the plug on the whole thing now."

Hunter and Grant exchanged a look that Kirk couldn't decipher. "Don't be so quick to call it quits," Grant said.

"What's the point of prolonging it? It's obvious that to her, we're already history."

Hunter drained his beer, a thoughtful expression on his face. "I think I have a handle on what you're going through, Kirk. I know what it's like to feel as if you have no control over your life." Dryly he added, "Looking at the engagement ring your brother bought for the woman you love will do that to you. There was a time when it looked like Raven was destined to be my sister-in-law, and there wasn't a damn thing I could do about it. Almost drove me out of my mind. And if you want to feel lower than pond scum, try sleeping with the woman your brother's set on marrying. That'll do the trick."

"But things worked out for you and Raven," Kirk said.

"They almost didn't. I felt so damn guilty for betraying Brent, I bolted. Hightailed it to Vermont and didn't tell anyone where I was going. Figured I was just in the way back home, messing things up for the happy couple."

Kirk snorted in derision. "You ran away when you should've stayed and fought for the woman you loved, come hell or high water."

"Like you're doing?"

Kirk's beer bottle stopped halfway to his mouth. "It's not the same thing. And anyway, I'm not going anywhere. Here I am and here I'll stay. For all the good it'll do me."

"That attitude isn't going to win her back," Grant said.

Kirk ran his fingers through his sweat-damp hair.

"Sunny knows how I feel about her. What more can I do?"

"You mean, besides passively sitting by while she convinces herself she's better off without you?" Grant asked.

"Letting her stew in her own resentment?" Hunter added. "Day after day?"

"I can't force Sunny to love me," Kirk snapped.

Grant laughed. "She already loves you! That woman's loved you for twelve years, you idiot!"

Kirk dropped his head in his hands. "Sometimes love's not enough."

Hunter said, "'You should've fought for the woman you loved.' Seems to me I heard those words recently."

"'Come hell or high water,'" Grant added. "I heard that, too. I believe it came from that pitiful specimen hanging his head over here."

Kirk looked at his friends. "Why is it so important that I not break up with Sunny? What is it that you're not telling me?"

Their look of studied innocence didn't fool him for a second, but it was clear that whatever intrigue was brewing, Kirk wouldn't get to the bottom of it today.

Besides, they were right. He wasn't going to win Sunny back by sitting around feeling sorry for himself.

Kirk had been scolded enough for one day. He came to his feet. "Let's get the rest of that drywall up."

9

FROM HER LOUNGING SPOT on a plastic lawn chair,
Sunny watched the back door of Charli's parents'
house swing open. She watched Charli elbow past
the screen door, carrying a hammered aluminum
tray laden with hot dog and hamburger buns, mus-
tard, ketchup, pickle relish and sauerkraut. Sunny
waited for her to notice what Amanda was doing to
Charli's grandmother.

"I hope I have enough—" Charli broke off with a
gasp. Two packs of hot dog buns slid off the tray
onto the grass. *"What are you doing to Nonni?"*

"Shh!" Amanda dipped the little brush into the
bottle of nail polish. "You'll wake her."

Amanda had pulled the picnic bench in front of
the cushioned lawn chair where Charli's grandmother was enthroned, her head tipped back, snoring like a handsaw. The well-padded ninety-three-
year-old matriarch of the Rossi family was clad in
her usual plain black dress, her iron-gray hair
yanked back into a high bun, her yamlike legs ending in sensible black shoes that dangled a couple of
inches above the grass.

Amanda was painting Mrs. Rossi's stubby fingernails from a tiny bottle labeled Siren Song, an eye-popping shade of frosted coral somewhere on the chromatic scale between slut fuchsia and working-girl orange. Amanda started in on the other hand, and Mrs. Rossi mumbled something in Italian, still sound asleep.

"No no no no no!" Charli whined, dumping the tray on the picnic table and rushing to Amanda. "You can't do that!"

Amanda ignored her friend's outburst. "Translate for me. Is she having a sexy dream?"

Charli's eyes narrowed dangerously. "Nonni said, 'When I wake up, I'm going to get my good friend Dominic "the Dentist" Giacopetti to do a little oral surgery on the no-good tramp making me look like a—'"

"I know, like a no-good tramp." Amanda leaned in close to Mrs. Rossi's plump fingers, propped on the armrest of her chair. "Does she really know guys like that?"

Sunny raised her hand, shielding her eyes from the bright sunlight. She grinned. "How badly do you want to find out?"

"You don't understand!" Charli hissed. "Nonni never wears cosmetics of any kind. She'll have a heart attack when she sees this." She wheeled on Sunny and Raven, calmly basking in the sun. "How could you let her do this?"

Raven chuckled. "Since when has anyone ever been able to stop Amanda from doing anything?"

"That color!" Charli groaned, slumping onto the bench next to Amanda.

"What's wrong with it?" Amanda tilted her head, regarding her work appraisingly. "I think it looks nice on her."

"Is it too much to hope you brought some polish remover, too?"

"Why would I schlepp around polish remover?"

"Great. I know for a fact there's none in the house." Charli stared balefully at her friend. "Back when Nonni was in the hospital for that angioplasty, I asked her if she'd like me to put a little clear polish on her nails. I thought it would cheer her up to be pampered. Do you know what she said?"

Amanda bent low to do the pinkie nail. "She said, 'Can that clear crap, I want me some dragon-lady press-ons!'"

"Yeah, right. Nonni scowled down her nose at me and said she'd never worn paint in her life and she wasn't going to start now." Charli gestured toward her grandmother's vivid manicure. "And look what you've done! The shock will put her back in the hospital for sure."

Raven said, "I don't think your grandmother is quite that fragile, Charli."

Like Sunny and Raven, Amanda had known Mrs. Rossi since she was five. During their school years and into adulthood, the girls had spent a lot of time at Charli's parents' house, sharing big Italian dinners, sleep-over parties and Charli's grandmother, who treated them all like members of the family. A lifelong confidante, Mrs. Rossi was the only person aside from Hunter and Grant who knew about the Wedding Ring the girls had established in their senior year of high school.

Despite the occasional acerbic exchange between Mrs. Rossi and the outspoken, twice-divorced Amanda, Sunny knew that deep down, Mrs. Rossi was as fond of her as she was of the others.

Amanda dropped the bottle of nail polish into her purse, lying at her feet. She blew lightly on the old woman's fingertips, causing her to jerk in her sleep. Charli clutched her chest.

Sunny pushed herself out of her chair and headed for the barbecue grill. "I bet those coals are ready." They were. "The hot dogs can go on last." As she placed spicy Italian sausages and thick burger patties on the grill, she asked, "Will someone set the table?"

"I'm already on it," Raven said, as she counted out paper plates.

Charli's grandmother snorted loudly and shifted in her chair. All eyes swung to her. Sunny knew she wasn't the only one holding her breath.

Mrs. Rossi opened her eyes, blinking against the sunlight. Glancing around, she took note of the four young women all staring at her. "Mmm, something smells good. That butcher in Lynbrook, he make the best *salciccia. Deliziosa!*" A gnat buzzed her face and absently she swatted it away. A funny little sound escaped Charli. Her grandmother, however, appeared oblivious to the beauty treatment she'd received while nestled in the arms of Morpheus.

"Um, Nonni..." Charli wore a weak smile. "You know, Amanda's such a kidder, heh heh. She did this silly thing—"

"She better not be silly when it's her turn for a husband!" Mrs. Rossi barked in her thick Italian accent. Sunny tried not to stare at the coral-tipped finger she wagged at Amanda. *"Due divorzi! E un disonore!"*

"I believe we've been over this ground before," Amanda responded in bored tones. "Marriage and I don't mix." To her friends she added, "I'm not going to go along with any matchmaking, so don't even bother trying."

"But we all agreed!" Charli said.

"We agreed back when we were dumb little teenagers with no life experience." Amanda rummaged in her purse and came up with a pair of designer sunglasses, which she slid onto her nose. "One thing my two strolls down the aisle have taught me is that I don't need a man's ring on my finger to find fulfillment. Sometimes it even gets in the way."

Amanda's remark about fulfillment struck a little close to home, being the exact opposite of the philosophy Sunny had adhered to for so long. Amanda was a successful business owner, the publisher of a popular and lucrative children's magazine. She'd studied journalism at Cornell University and started her own publication on a shoestring within five years of graduating. Her career gave her enormous satisfaction. Sunny, in comparison, came off as a real loser, the "resident underachiever," as she'd once described herself to Kirk.

Over the years, Sunny had toyed with the idea of taking courses at a local college, not toward a degree necessarily, but just for her personal enjoyment and to learn more about subjects that interested her. She'd always been fascinated by local Long Island history, for example.

And archaeology. One of her regulars at the diner had told her about a program through Garrison University in which laypeople got to excavate an ancient Native American site located in a state park. The idea of doing that sort of work had fired her imagination, but Sunny had never thought of herself as the kind of person who did such things. She was just a high school graduate, after all, biding her time until she achieved her ultimate goal of a husband and children.

That was the niche she'd placed herself in, but she had to admit, the niche had grown confining over the years. Nowhere in her limited self-definition was there room for intellectual curiosity or mental challenge.

And why shouldn't there be? If her experience with Kirk had given her nothing else of worth, at least he'd forced her to admit that her longtime goal was not incompatible with personal fulfillment. She could—and should—have both. Tomorrow she'd call Garrison and request a catalog of continuing-education courses. With any luck, she'd still be able to register for the fall semester.

"Little bird," Mrs. Rossi said, calling Raven by her pet name for her. "You're three months along, *sì*? But so flat still! Where is that *bambino*?"

Raven pressed her hands to her middle, outlining the gentle mound hiding under her low-waisted sundress. "It's there, Mrs. Rossi. And getting bigger every day."

"You make sure you eat. These doctors nowadays, not letting the mamas gain enough weight. *Ridicolo!* What do they know?"

During this tirade, Mrs. Rossi gesticulated like the Italian she was, those hot coral fingernails flashing in the sunlight. Sunny's heart couldn't stand it. She had to look away.

Observing the progress of Raven's pregnancy was a bittersweet experience for Sunny. She was happy for her friend, happy that she'd found the man she was meant to share her life with, happy that they were soon to be blessed with their first child. But at the same time, Raven's experience highlighted all that had gone disastrously wrong in Sunny's life.

She turned to her friends. "I have to stop seeing Kirk." She didn't have to say why. They all knew what she'd found out about him three days earlier.

Charli adopted a mulish expression. Of the four of them, she took their matchmaking pact the most to heart. It was a sacred vow, in her view, one not to be treated lightly. Amanda and Raven, and even Mrs. Rossi, looked like they'd expected this move.

"Now, hear me out," Sunny said. "I know I'm supposed to stick with it for a whole three months, but you can't hold me to that. Not after what I've learned."

"I don't see that that changes anything," Charli said.

"It doesn't change anything?" Sunny flipped hamburgers with unnecessary zeal. "I went into that relationship under false pretenses! He deceived me! That automatically invalidates the deal."

"Show me that in the rule book," Amanda drawled.

"There is no rule book," Sunny retorted.

Amanda shrugged.

"You know," Raven said, "it really doesn't matter that Kirk was concealing the truth. He's the man we picked, so he's the man you're obligated to date for the required period of time, false pretenses or no."

"Unless he calls it off," Amanda said. "Has he?"

"No. Not yet."

Charli said, "And no fair trying to make him do it."

"Another one of those convenient rules we never agreed on?" Amanda asked.

"What?" Charli turned to Amanda. "You want her to be able to squirm out of it?"

"Not me." Amanda held up her hands. "Make up all the rules you want."

Raven said, "I was the first one to try to squirm out of it, you know. When Brent took my unwillingness to sleep with him as an excuse to cheat on me."

"And I defended you!" Sunny gestured with the spatula she held. "I said that since you had a relationship with Hunter, you shouldn't have to stick it out with his brother."

"Only I didn't have a relationship with Hunter at that point," Raven said. "His strong sense of family loyalty wouldn't allow it. What I'm saying is, you guys didn't let me off the hook. You knew things had to run their course. You knew it would all work out in the end."

"Not me," Amanda said. "I figured it was a losing proposition all around."

Raven turned to Amanda. "You know, you don't always have to say what's on your mind."

"Oh, okay, I'll try to exercise a little restraint," Amanda said, deadpan, before cracking up at the absurdity of the notion.

Charli glanced at her grandmother's startling manicure. "Nonni, I, uh, want to tell you something so it doesn't come as too much of a surprise."

"I know." The old woman gestured airily. "You and Grant, you're trying to make a *bambino*."

Charli gaped at her. "How did you know that? Did Grant tell you?"

"No one has to tell Luisa Rossi." She pointed to her own eye. "She sees. She sees how you and your handsome husband look at each other when you're around your little twin grandnieces. You think after ninety-three years your old Nonni doesn't know the signs?"

Charli sighed. "I didn't want to make some kind of big announcement that we were trying, in case it takes a while. Or in case it *doesn't* take."

Mrs. Rossi cackled. "If I didn't have this arthritis, I'd already be sewing the receiving blankets." As she said this, she rubbed her gnarled knuckles. Sunny thought for sure she'd spot Amanda's handiwork, but she never glanced down at her fingers as she told her granddaughter, "This time next year, you'll be cuddling your own *bambino.* I only hope I'm still around to see it."

No one bothered to respond to that last, wistful statement. Mrs. Rossi had been bemoaning her imminent demise since before Sunny and the others had been born, and would no doubt do so for many years to come.

"Look, Sunny," Raven said, "we all know this thing with Kirk is a terrible shock, but think about what you'd be giving up if you ended it now. In all other respects, he's perfect for you."

"What's the use in postponing the inevitable?" Exchanging the spatula for long-handled tongs, Sunny turned the links of Italian sausage, wonderfully aromatic and striped with grill marks. "Nothing can come of this relationship."

"Raven's right," Charli said. "You need a chance to come to terms with this whole thing. You need time to think about it. Instead of impulsively calling it—"

"Impulsive?" Sunny gestured broadly with tongs. "You've known me my whole life, practically. What's the one thing I've always wanted? The *only* thing I've wanted? This is not some impulsive whim!"

Charli looked pained. "I didn't mean that. I..."

"Is it too much to ask for?" Sunny's voice had turned shrill; tears of anger and frustration filmed her eyes. "A family of my own. Children! I envy you, Raven. I'm jealous of what you have, and I don't like feeling that way. I don't like being the kind of person who—" Her voice broke. "I love you, Raven, you know that. I really am thrilled for you and Hunter. I just..."

"I know, honey." Raven wrapped her arms around Sunny and hugged her tightly. "I know." After a few moments she pulled back and looked at her. "There are other ways."

Sunny wiped a tear off her cheek. She took a deep breath. "Adoption's not for me."

"Have you really thought about it?" Amanda asked. "I mean, what I'm hearing sounds like a knee-jerk reaction. An adopted child would be just as much your own as—"

"I know that," Sunny said tightly. "And no, I haven't really thought about it because I've always known just what I want. And that's not it."

The others exchanged a look. Charli said, "Maybe

you should kind of expand your thinking at this point, consider things you never did before. Rather than give up a good man who loves you."

How could Sunny make them understand? If her lifelong dream could never be fulfilled, then her life up to that point would have been a waste. All her sacrifices, all those years putting her mind on hold and running herself ragged at Wafflemania—all of it would have been for nothing. Sunny didn't think she could face that.

As she transferred the burgers to a platter and put the hot dogs on to cook, she said, "You know, whatever the rest of you wanted in life, you went after. And got. Your careers, all that. You didn't lower your standards, your expectations. Why should I?"

Mrs. Rossi spoke up. "How about a sperm bank?" The four young women stared at her. "I saw it on *Dateline*. The sperm, it comes from a medical student, a nice boy from a good *famiglia*. The mama, she give birth, not like adoption. It's a good, uh..." As she groped for the right word, she twirled her hand in front of her face, somehow blind to Amanda's Day-Glo paint job. "*Compromesso*."

"Compromise," Charli translated.

"*Sì*, compromise. It's a good compromise," she told Sunny with a brisk nod. "You do this."

As far as Mrs. Rossi was concerned, the issue was clearly settled. Problem solved.

"I appreciate the suggestion," Sunny said, "but it isn't the same. To me, a child represents the ultimate union of a man and a woman—part me, part the man I love." In a small voice she added, "I guess I'm just not ready to compromise on something so important to me."

Quietly Raven said, "There's Ian."

Something squeezed hard inside Sunny's chest. "Ian's a great kid. You know how much I...I love him."

"And he loves you, too," Charli said. "Anyone can see that."

Sunny didn't want to think about how close she and Kirk's son had already become. He'd lost his mother, and now he was going to lose her. The best thing she could do for Ian now was to keep her distance. To let him forget her.

Mrs. Rossi didn't pull any punches. "That boy needs a mama."

"Don't do that to me," Sunny pleaded. "That isn't what this is about."

"It's part of what it's about," Charli said.

"He's—he's not my responsibility," Sunny said, trying to put conviction in her voice, hating her friends in that moment for making her say these things, think these things. "If what Kirk wants is just a stand-in mother for his son, he's picked the wrong woman."

"Is that what he wants?" Raven asked.

Sunny couldn't lie. "No. I mean, I think he'd be happy if Ian had two parents, but that isn't what this relationship is about for him. He wants me for me."

Amanda pulled off her sunglasses and looked her in the eye, and in that instant Sunny glimpsed the vulnerability her friend kept so deeply hidden, the legacy of two disastrous marriages. "Do you have any idea how lucky you are?" she asked.

"Is 'lucky' supposed to hurt this much?" Sunny looked at each woman in turn. "Are you really going to put me through five more weeks of this?"

Raven said, "Something tells me Kirk is hurting, too. Sunny, if we didn't feel so strongly that the two of you need each other, it would be different."

"So there will be no reprieve," Sunny said.

"You make it sound like we're sticking bamboo shoots under your fingernails," Amanda stated. "We're only holding you to the agreement you freely made."

"Ha!" Mrs. Rossi stabbed her finger at Amanda. "You made the agreement, too. So don't say, 'No husband for me.'"

Amanda smiled serenely. "How do you like your manicure, Mrs. Rossi?"

Sunny's heart flipped over as Charli's grandmother splayed her fingers in front of her face and inspected them. Her expression never changed. "It's growing on me."

"Nonni!" Charli stared slack-jawed at her grandmother. "You noticed?"

"You think I could sleep with all of you yap-yap-yapping like *gazzas*?" Mrs. Rossi made talking motions with her hand. "I knew what this one was up to," she said, jerking her head toward Amanda.

"Well, now that you've gotten over the shock—" Amanda smirked at the others "—what do you think of the color?"

The old woman examined her nails again. "Eh. What else you got?"

"I don't believe this," Charli muttered. "You wouldn't even let me put a coat of clear on your nails, Nonni."

Sunny smiled wryly. "I think your mistake was asking, Charli."

Amanda reached into her purse and dumped a multicolored assortment of little bottles on Mrs. Rossi's lap. "You look these over while I strip off this color." She produced a bottle of nail-polish remover and some cotton balls. "What do you think of the brick-red?"

"You!" Outraged color flooded Charli's face. "You told me you didn't have any remover!"

"No, she didn't," Mrs. Rossi corrected as she pawed through the bottles. "She said, 'Why would I schlepp it around?' What are dragon-lady press-ons?" she asked Amanda.

"I'll bring some next time."

10

EXITING Garrison University's physics building, Kirk left the walking path and cut across the lawn toward the ivy-covered main library. Now that the fall semester was in full swing, the campus was a swarm of noise and activity, with students hurrying from classrooms and labs to dormitories, dining halls, the student union and various libraries. It was late afternoon, the day warm but overcast, the air thick with the promise of rain.

Kirk had had misgivings about leaving his position at prestigious Stanford University to teach here at Garrison. After all, Garrison couldn't hope to pull in the kinds of donations and endowments enjoyed by the larger institutions. Likewise, it struggled to attract the highest echelon of students, the brilliant young minds that flocked to the Ivies and the better-known research universities—the kind of student Kirk himself had once been.

But what Garrison lacked in funds and prestige, it made up for in other ways. Classes were kept small; undergraduates were taught by full professors rather than grad students, and had ample opportunity to engage in research. Some exciting, innovative work was being quietly conducted behind these venerable redbrick walls.

And while Garrison's administration liked to see its faculty members' names in the journals, the emphasis was on teaching rather than publishing. Kirk's office was across the hall from the classrooms where he taught; his students had plenty of access to him.

All in all, this major move, while prompted by tragedy and loss, was turning into one of the best decisions he'd ever made.

Kirk's thoughts were interrupted by a glimpse of long, reddish-brown hair at the periphery of his vision. *Sunny,* he thought, even as he told himself he was mistaken. It was some girl with similar hair; it had to be. He squinted into the distant crowd of students, lost sight of her, shook his head at his foolishness and continued on his way.

The knot of students parted and there she was, his Sunny. He stopped dead in his tracks, staring as she strode briskly in the direction he'd come from. She wore an Asian-print T-shirt tucked into baggy denim cargo shorts, and had her leather backpack purse slung over one shoulder.

"Sunny!" She didn't hear him. Loping toward her, he cupped his hands around his mouth and bellowed, "Sunny!"

She slowed and glanced around, finally spotting Kirk, who quickly closed the distance between them. He knew he was wearing a stupid grin, but he couldn't help it. He hadn't seen her since last Saturday, another of those tiresome double dates she now insisted on so the two of them wouldn't have to engage in any meaningful communication. He and Sunny hadn't been alone together since he'd told her about his vasectomy two weeks earlier.

"You almost missed me," he said. "My last class just ended. I'm on my way to the library. There's a great little bistro there—I'll buy you some cappuccino and cherry cheesecake." He urged her along with a hand to her waist, but she stood rooted to the spot.

"Kirk, I didn't come here looking for you."

For an instant it was as if she were speaking in a foreign tongue. What business could Sunny Bleecker have on campus that didn't involve him?

His confounded expression wasn't lost on her. Her features hardened, just a bit, and it struck Kirk that somehow he'd managed to insult her.

"I registered for a course," she said. "There's this archaeological project where you help excavate a Native American village."

"Yeah, I, uh, think I heard about that." Kirk was still mentally off balance, but he quickly recovered. "It's through the archaeology department here. Who heads up that project?"

"Monica Goldfarb."

"I haven't met her, but I've heard good things about her."

Sunny glanced toward her destination—the social

sciences building, just past the physics building—clearly impatient to be on her way. "I have to pick up some materials, and Dr. Goldfarb's assistant is going to meet with me to get me caught up. Basically it's a summer program, but there are still a few weeks of digging left and a couple of people had to quit, so they're letting me join late."

"That's great. That's really... I never knew you were interested in that stuff."

"I'm interested in a lot of things."

"Well, yeah, of course you are. I guess I'm just surprised to see you, you know..."

She smiled without humor. "Improving my mind?"

"No. That's not what I meant."

"I found out I can audit courses, too. Just sit in without earning credit. I'm thinking of doing that with a couple of history courses—if they're given at the right times. I already had to rearrange my work schedule for the archaeology project. Mike gave me a hard time about it," she said, referring to her boss at Wafflemania, "but I can handle him. After twelve years of being his most reliable waitress, I'm entitled to some concessions."

"So. You're going to college."

"Well, sort of."

"Maybe one day you'd like to go for your B.A. You can do that part-time, you know. You don't have to quit your job."

"I think I'll see how this works out first," Sunny said, but he could tell the idea had occurred to her.

This conversation was typical of their interactions the past two weeks, Kirk thought, civil and even friendly, but a far cry from their previous warm intimacy. It was as if they'd never made love, as if they'd never lain in bed half the night discussing their deepest fears and desires. They could have been two casual acquaintances. Kirk couldn't help but wonder if this was how amicably divorced couples dealt with each other.

During the several dates they'd had since she'd learned his secret, Kirk had respected Sunny's decision to remain platonic—not that they'd had the opportunity to be anything but, always being in the company of others. He was frustrated, both emotionally and physically. He'd hoped that by this point she'd have thought things through and concluded that their relationship meant too much to her to walk away from.

He'd done his damnedest to sway her in that direction, but since she actively avoided being alone with him, and wouldn't even stay on the phone more than a minute or two at a shot, his efforts had met with little success.

He said, "I'll walk with you."

"Oh, that's not necessary. I—"

"What do you think I'm going to do to you in this crowd of people?" Exasperated, he started walking, and glanced back to see her resigned expression as she reluctantly caught up to him.

After a few moments Kirk said, "Ian's been asking for you."

Her gaze snapped to his, and in the fleeting instant before she turned away, he saw the aching loss she couldn't hide.

"I know you care about him," he said.

"Of course I care about Ian." Sunny's forced nonchalance didn't fool Kirk for an instant.

"He's confused. He asks for you, and I don't know what to tell him."

Kirk wondered if Sunny was aware of how much her expressive features mirrored her internal struggle.

"Tell him..." She broke off with a ragged sigh. "You don't have to tell him anything. He'll forget me soon enough."

Kirk stumbled to a stop. Sunny resolutely kept walking. "Why, Sunny?"

She took another few steps and stopped, her back to him, her entire body tense. After a moment she turned, and the bleakness in her eyes told him more than he wanted to know.

Slowly he approached her, not wanting to make this discussion public as student traffic flowed past on all sides. "You're planning to end it," he said, "I know you are. So what are you waiting for? Why keep me hanging on? Hoping?"

"It's not...I can't. I can't just break up."

"I never thought of you as indecisive," he said, "or the kind of manipulative woman who maneuvers the guy into doing the deed."

She studied the grass at her feet. "I can't explain it."

"Well, whatever caused the state of limbo we find ourselves in, I seem to be the only one who hasn't been let in on it."

Her head came up. "What do you mean?"

"It's like there's some kind of secret society that knows more about our relationship than I do. Or did you think I'm too dense to pick up on the weird signals I'm getting? Grant and Hunter seem dead set on keeping me from breaking it off with you."

Sunny's eyes widened; Kirk hadn't known she could look so vulnerable. "You wanted to break up?"

"When it's obvious you're just going through the motions? Don't tell me you're surprised."

After a moment she said, "I guess I'm not."

"Look." He glanced around at the throng of people passing by. "Let's take this conversation somewhere private."

Sunny started to shake her head. Kirk grabbed her arm and propelled her toward the physics building, which they were passing en route to social sciences. "Why are you so determined not to be alone with me?" he asked. "Afraid your resolve might weaken? Afraid you might have to acknowledge—to me and to yourself—just how much we mean to each other?"

She tried to twist away from him as they passed through the front entrance of the physics building. He wouldn't let her. She said, "I have to meet with—"

"Goldfarb's assistant can wait. This won't take long. There's something we need to discuss."

Sunny's look of alarm would have been funny if it weren't so telling. Clearly, the last thing she wanted was meaningful communication with him, anything that would make it harder to distance herself from him.

"Where are we going?" she asked as he directed her up the stairs to the third floor.

He didn't respond until they were in the large classroom where he taught thermodynamics. His scrawled equations still adorned the large chalkboard, facing his lab table and the rows of tables and chairs where his students sat. He nodded toward the nearest chair. "Have a seat."

Sunny remained standing; she folded her arms. "I'm not some intimidated little freshman, Professor Larsen, so just say what you have to say."

"I'm thinking of having my vasectomy reversed."

She stared mutely for a few seconds, then plopped down into the chair he'd offered. He sat next to her, but said nothing, just let her absorb his words.

He watched hope spread across her face. He heard it in her voice when she said, "I didn't know they could do that."

"It's a delicate microsurgical procedure. It takes

about three hours, according to this doctor I talked to—a lot longer than the vasectomy did. But the thing is, reversal isn't always successful."

A burst of raucous conversation came from the hallway as a cluster of students passed the room. Kirk got up and closed the door, then returned to the seat next to Sunny's.

She looked at him. "What are the chances of success? Did he say?"

"Pretty high in my case, because it was done only ten months ago. It seems the longer you wait, the less likely they'll be able to reverse it."

She chewed her lip. "So it'll probably work, but it's not a sure thing."

"Right. And I've got to tell you, Sunny, this operation is expensive, about four thousand dollars."

"That's a lot of money."

"And my medical insurance won't pay for it. I'll have to borrow the cash. I've put all my savings into this move and the house. I'm tapped out."

"But if the surgery works..."

"If it works, it'll be worth every penny. I'm willing to go into debt and go through this whole thing, even knowing it may not work, but I need something from you before I do it."

She waited for him to continue.

Kirk took Sunny's hand. "I need to know that we're in this together. That you're committed to me regardless of the outcome."

Reflexively she tried to pull her hand away. He held on tight. "Sunny, look at me."

She did.

"I know how important it is to you," he said quietly. "Becoming a mother."

"I know you know. It's why you..." Her features tightened in pain.

"It's why I let you believe I could still father children. That was wrong of me. I shouldn't have done it. The reason I did...Sunny, I was so afraid of losing you." With a lopsided smile he added, "Something tells me I'm not the first guy who did something stupid because he was hopelessly in love."

She took an unsteady breath and let it out. "I wish...I wish we knew for sure that this operation would work."

"Listen to me," he said. "You and me, we're about *you and me*. Having a child with you would be, well, it would be incredible, I won't deny it. But even if that's not meant to be, we can still have a wonderful life together."

Her eyes briefly closed, as if she were shoring up her defenses. "To me, a wonderful life means—"

"I know. It means a family of your own. A man who cherishes you and a bunch of kids who look like you and him."

She was surprised to hear it put so succinctly, he could tell. Perhaps she was surprised that he understood her so well.

"Sometimes," he said, "life throws us a curve ball. We have to alter our plans."

"Charli said something like that," she murmured.

"Take me, for example. I had the life I'd always wanted in California. I had this great job teaching at Stanford, everything was wonderful—just like I'd planned. Then I lost Linda and my world bottomed out. I knew I needed a radical change—just like I knew Ian needed something more than I could give him out there—so I pulled up stakes and uprooted us. I was worried that maybe I was making the worst mistake of my life, but it turned out to be just what we needed." He gave her a significant look. "For me as much as for Ian. I wouldn't have met you again if I'd stayed out there."

"You can't compare our experiences," Sunny said. "You're still doing what you love—teaching college—just in a different place. No one asked you to redefine what it took to make you happy. No one suggested that maybe you should give up physics and teach English literature. Or teach elementary school kids. Or do research for some company instead of teaching. The only thing that's changed for you is the setting."

"All I'm asking is for you to consider alternatives."

"God, I hate that word," she muttered. "I don't want to hear any more about *alternatives*. Adoption. Artificial insemination."

He couldn't restrain a smile. "Raven and Charli

and Amanda have been offering pearls of wisdom, have they?"

"Along with Mrs. Rossi."

"Charli's mother?"

"Her grandmother. She was the one who suggested I use a sperm bank."

Kirk had met Charli's grandmother. He tried to imagine that conversation and failed miserably.

"I'm willing to go any route that you're comfortable with," he said. "If you change your mind and want to try adoption, whatever. As long as we're together."

"I...I don't think I'll change my mind about that."

"Well, that leaves the reversal surgery."

She wouldn't meet his eyes.

"I meant what I said," he continued. "Before I take this step—before I go under the knife for an expensive procedure that may or may not work—I need to know that our future together doesn't hinge on whether we can make babies."

He watched competing emotions battle it out behind her eyes. The longer he waited for a response, the more he felt hope drifting away from him. Sunny looked down at their linked hands, and only then did he realize how tightly he was squeezing her fingers. He let go.

"I wish I could give you that assurance," she said, her eyes fixed on her lap. "I can't."

A heavy silence settled between them, punctuated

by the muffled sounds of conversation elsewhere in the building.

Kirk's throat felt constricted. "Do you need more time? To think about it?"

Mutely she shook her head, then abruptly grabbed her purse and leaped to her feet. Her voice was hoarse with unshed tears. "I have to go."

Before he could respond, she was out the door.

SUNNY STOOD in the open doorway of her apartment just after 11:00 p.m. Kirk had just buzzed her from the lobby, interrupting her perusal of the archaeology notes Dr. Goldfarb's assistant had given her that afternoon. She tightened the sash of her pink-and-white seersucker bathrobe, closing it more firmly over her nightgown.

She was staring in the direction of the elevators when she heard a grating noise as the fire door leading to the stairway at the end of the hallway opened behind her. She turned to see Kirk emerge, drenched to the skin. The thunderstorm that had been threatening all day had finally struck around dinnertime, and it had yet to let up. He'd climbed the four flights of stairs, apparently too impatient to wait for the elevator.

"Kirk, is something wrong?" she asked as he joined her at the entrance to her apartment. He hadn't called to let her know he was on his way, had simply shown up unannounced.

"We need to talk," he said.

"We talked earlier. I told you, I can't—"

"I know what you said. This won't take long."

Sunny swallowed hard. Something about his flat tone of voice, the hard set of his features, sent a shiver of unease down her spine. "What is it?"

"Not out here."

"Kirk, it's late. I...I was getting ready for bed," she lied. "You said it won't take long, so just tell me—"

He pushed past her into the apartment and stood in her foyer, dripping rainwater on her floral-patterned area rug. Sunny followed him inside and closed the door.

She asked, "What's so important that—"

"It's over, Sunny."

Something kicked in her chest, hard. She should have expected it, *had* expected it, but now that it had actually happened...

Sunny tried to force words up her throat, some kind of rational response, but nothing came.

Kirk wiped his palm over his face and pushed his fingers through his sodden hair. "You know this isn't what I want," he continued, "but what I want doesn't seem to make a damn bit of difference."

She struggled to regulate her breathing, to maintain her dignity. "This isn't what I..." She didn't finish. How could she stand there and tell him this wasn't what she wanted, either, when her actions of the past two weeks said otherwise? If not for the Wedding Ring's three-month rule, she would have broken up with Kirk the night she'd learned the truth about him.

"I can't do this anymore." Kirk spread his arms. "I can't invest myself emotionally in a relationship that no longer exists. I've just been fooling myself."

"We...we have a relationship, Kirk."

He studied her expression. What did he see? She looked away.

"Do we?" he said quietly. "You've closed yourself off to me, Sunny. Nothing I do seems to get through. I've apologized for deceiving you. I've tried to give you time. Time to get over the shock, to come to grips with it. And to realize what you're throwing away."

She leaned back against the door, her legs too shaky to support her. She whispered, "It's more complicated than you know."

A wry expression twisted his features. "Yeah, I'm getting that."

Thunder rumbled in the distance. Moments later, lightning flashed in the night sky beyond the living room windows.

She said, "This isn't what I wanted, Kirk."

"I know what you wanted. You wanted the dream family you've been fixated on since you were a teenager. You want all the pieces to fall neatly into place."

"Stop it."

"But life isn't like that. Shitty things happen, and you have to roll with the punches or you'll be left with nothing."

Sunny's chin wobbled. "I'm not asking for anything special. I only want what everyone else takes for granted."

"'Everyone else'? Don't you know that a significant percentage of married couples have fertility problems? Or haven't you heard all the hoopla about in vitro and surrogate mothers and—"

"You make me sound selfish for just wanting—" She broke off with a sob.

"Sunny." Kirk tried to hold her, but she stiffened and pulled away, keeping the tears at bay with a supreme effort.

He sighed. "Sunny, I love you. I love you so much it's ripping me apart. If it were in my power to give you everything your heart desires—be it a houseful of children or the moon and the stars—I'd gladly do it. But I'm just a man. I've made choices. Choices that were carefully thought out, choices I felt were right at the time. I may not be able to give you babies, but I can give you a lifetime of love. Enduring, exclusive, unconditional love."

He opened the door and turned back to her one last time. "If you decide that's enough, then you know where to find me."

11

"SUNNY, thank God you're home. Let me talk to Kirk."

The caller didn't identify herself, but Sunny recognized the voice on the phone. It was Kirk's mother. "Marianne, he's not here. What's wrong?"

"He's not there? But he said... Just a second, sweetheart, Grandma's trying to find Daddy."

Marianne was obviously addressing Ian. Sunny heard him whining for his father, practically into the receiver of the phone. Marianne must have been holding him with her free arm. Something in Ian's voice kicked Sunny's blood pressure up. She heard panic, and pain.

"Sunny, he has to be with you. He said he had a date in the city. I called your number thinking I'd leave a message on your machine and you'd retrieve it from wherever and he'd call back."

"Marianne, I haven't seen Kirk since Wednesday." Not since that stormy night when he broke up with her—a fact he obviously hadn't shared with his parents. That had been a mere three days earlier, and already he was dating someone else. Sunny tucked away that depressing fact to brood over later, and forced herself to focus on the reason for Marianne's frantic call.

Ian.

"He's not with you?" Marianne said. "Then who—" She stopped abruptly.

Sunny waited out the awkward conversational gap while Kirk's mother mentally filled in the blanks.

"We broke up," Sunny said.

"I—I didn't know. He didn't tell me."

"Well..." Sunny sighed. What could she say to that? "What's wrong with Ian?" His complaints were increasing in pitch and volume.

"Oh, I don't know. I'm so upset. Yes, honey, Daddy will be home soon, it's all right, sweetheart." To Sunny she said, "It's something with his arm. He's holding it and he's obviously in pain—"

"Hold on." Sunny tamped down her mounting anxiety; it wouldn't help Ian to have every adult in the vicinity panicking. She racked her brain. What were the warning signs of serious injury? "Is the arm swollen?"

"Uh, no. No, it looks normal. But he keeps babying it. Actually, it may be the shoulder that hurts him, or the wrist. I can't tell for sure, the way he's holding it—"

"Is it discolored?" Sunny was pacing the length of her bedroom, with her cordless phone pressed to her ear.

"Discolored? No. That's the first thing I looked for."

"Not swollen or discolored, I'm thinking it's probably not broken. How long has he been complaining?"

"About twenty minutes. Oh, it's all my fault! I was holding him by the hand. We'd been to the library—he loves playing with the puzzles there and looking at the picture books. Anyway, we were coming back up the front porch steps and he was kind of fussy. It was past his naptime—you know how he gets, how he kind of balks and tries to pull away?"

"Yes, I know. Marianne, just tell me what happened." *Patience*, Sunny cautioned herself. Ian's shrill pleas for his "da" ripped right through her.

"Well, he just sat down suddenly—boom! Right on his fanny, while I was still holding his arm. And then it started hurting him, and it's all my fault! I must've been holding him too tight, or pulling too hard, or—"

"It's not your fault, Marianne! I'm sure it's nothing too serious. Is Fred there?" Sunny asked, referring to Kirk's father.

"No, he went fishing with Stu Baumgarten. I'm here alone with Ian."

"At your house?"

"No, at Kirk's."

"Ian has to see a doctor."

"I know that, but I just thought if I could get hold of Kirk first..."

"We can't wait for him. Ian needs to be looked at right away. I'd like to avoid the emergency room if we can."

"Oh God! The emergency room! Those places are packed on weekends!"

"Listen." Sunny stopped pacing to sit on her bed and shove her bare feet into sneakers. "Do you know if Ian's pediatrician sees patients on Saturday?"

"I—I don't know, but I have his number right here."

"Well, call and find out." Sunny clamped the phone between her jaw and shoulder as she tied her shoelaces. "I'm on my way over. I'll be there in under ten minutes. Wait for me."

"I can call a taxi." Kirk's mother didn't drive.

"No! Wait for me. I'll be right there."

"YOU'RE RIGHT, it's not swollen or discolored," Sunny murmured to Marianne, as she carefully examined Ian's arm. As gentle as her touch was, he whined and pulled away. He kept the arm close to his body, the elbow slightly bent, supporting its weight with his other hand.

"Ian, I know it hurts." Sunny sat on Kirk's living room sofa, with the boy on her lap. "It's an owie, isn't it?" she asked sympathetically, using the term he was accustomed to.

He nodded. "Owie."

A surge of protectiveness welled up inside Sunny, of a magnitude she'd never felt before. In that instant she knew she wouldn't rest until he was all better. Thank goodness Ian's pediatrician was still in the office. He'd been about to leave for the day when Marianne had called. He'd promised to wait for their arrival.

"I'm going to take you to the doctor," she told Ian. "Dr. Davidson. You like Dr. Davidson, don't you?"

He shook his head, scowling. "Owie."

Marianne explained. "Ian had a vaccination a couple of weeks ago."

"Well, I don't think you're going to get a shot today. Dr. Davidson is going to look at your arm and make it all better." *Please let it be true*, she prayed as she stood up with the little boy in her arms.

Marianne said, "Kirk left Ian's booster seat for the car. I'll bring it outside for you."

As Marianne positioned the elevated seat in the back of Sunny's five-year-old Corolla, she said, "I keep paging Kirk, but he hasn't responded. I can't imagine why."

One obvious reason pounced into Sunny's consciousness before she had a chance to leash it. You wouldn't hear the beeping of the pager clipped to your belt if you were nowhere near your clothes, now would you?

The image of Kirk writhing naked in some bed with some other woman planted itself in Sunny's mind like a burr. *Let it go*, she told herself firmly. *Just get Ian through this. Later, when this is all over, you can feel sorry for yourself all you want.*

"Kirk always calls when he's out, several times," Marianne said from the interior of the Corolla's back seat, where she was positioning the booster. "Well, you know. He checks up on Ian constantly."

It was true. Sunny used to tease him for being overprotective. "But today?" she asked.

"Today—" Marianne let out a shout as she straightened out of the car, having smacked her head on the door frame. Rubbing her scalp, she said, "Today I told him not to call. I was very firm about it. 'Just have a good time,' I told him. 'You have the beeper. It's not like I can't get ahold of you if I need you.'" Helplessly she lifted her hands and let them drop. "But I've been trying and trying to get in touch with him. This is all my—"

"No more of that!" Sunny strapped Ian into the booster seat, murmuring reassurances to him. She kissed his forehead and closed the car door. Then she gave Kirk's mother a much-needed bear hug. "You didn't do anything wrong, Marianne, you hear me? You did everything right, including calling me."

Marianne's eyes misted. "God bless you, Sunny. I don't know what I would've done if you hadn't been home." She started to open the passenger door.

"No, you've got to stay here." Sunny slid behind the wheel. "In case Kirk calls."

"Oh. Yes, I suppose someone has to stay near the phone." Anxiously she looked from Sunny to Ian. "Are you sure you don't need me...?"

"Of course I'm sure." Sunny started the engine.

She forced a confident smile onto her face. "If Kirk does call, tell him everything's under control."

"CAN YOU DO THIS?" Dr. Davidson bent his own wrist back and forth.

Ian, perched on the examining table, shook his head.

"How about this?" The young doctor wiggled his fingers.

"Uh-uh."

"He can't move his hand?" Sunny asked, as alarm spiked.

"Oh, I'm sure he can, but it hurts, so he won't try. That's okay, you don't have to," he told the toddler with a warm smile as he continued to gently manipulate the arm. As before, Ian complained loudly, refusing to let his palm be turned forward.

"What's wrong with his hand?" Sunny heard the panic that infected her voice. "Is it sprained? It can't be broken, can it?"

"No, no, it's not broken. And it's not the hand, it's the elbow."

"The elbow?"

"Nursemaid's elbow, it's called. It's dislocated. The head of the radius, one of the bones in the arm, had slipped out of position. A very common childhood injury, especially for this age group."

"Oh." Dr. Davidson's calm manner helped to quell Sunny's anxiety. "What caused it?"

"Why don't you have a seat right here?" The doctor indicated a chair and lifted Ian onto Sunny's lap once she was settled in it. "Well, you said he sat down suddenly when his grandmother was holding his arm?"

"That's right."

Dr. Davidson shifted Ian's position a little. "Then that's when it happened. His arm was hyperextended and the ligament got stretched too far. Like I said, it's very common. It can happen when kids play, roughhouse, when they fall...." He smiled knowingly. "It's not Grandma's fault."

Sunny couldn't help returning his smile. "Try telling Grandma that. What's the treatment?"

"I'm going to pop that sucker back in place."

Sunny felt her eyes grow round. "Now?"

"Now." Dr. Davidson palpated the dislocated elbow joint. "If you stay calm, so will Ian. He won't be thrilled about this, but it'll be over real quick."

She responded with a weak smile and a nod. Her arms tightened around the little boy who'd come to mean so much to her in two short months.

The doctor was as good as his word. In one swift motion he manipulated the elbow back into position. Ian shouted, more in surprise, it seemed, than pain. One little holler and it was over. No tears, no tantrums.

Dr. Davidson praised his patient's bravery. Ian started moving the arm almost immediately, obviously free of pain. Sunny was stunned. That one simple maneuver had done the trick?

"Doesn't he need X rays?" she asked.

"Does he look like he needs X rays?"

She turned to Ian. "How's your owie?"

"Aw gone." He demonstrated it by wiggling the arm around.

"So that's it?" Sunny asked the doctor. "He's good as new?"

"Just about. No permanent harm was done, but you should be aware that since the ligament has been stretched, there's an increased chance of this happening again. Be careful not to pull on his hand. When you lift him, grasp him under the arms or around the body. And no swinging him by the arms."

"I-keam!" Ian crowed.

"You want ice cream?" She chuckled, as much in relief as amusement at the child's sudden shift in priorities. "Does Daddy buy you ice cream when you've been to the doctor?"

Ian nodded vigorously. "Shockit ship!"

"Mmm, my favorite, too," Dr. Davidson said.

Sunny gave Ian a big hug. "We'll stop on the way home and pick up chocolate chip ice cream—and maybe some fudge syrup and whipped cream, too."

12

WHILE ALLISON HYDE studied the painting on the wall of the SoHo gallery, Kirk studied her profile. She really was very pretty, a tall brunette with a nice figure and high cheekbones. A few years older than he was, but that didn't bother him. He'd noticed her his first day teaching at Garrison, though, of course, he'd done nothing about it because he'd been seeing Sunny at the time.

Allison taught art history, and so their paths hadn't crossed all that often, but when they had, he'd found himself gently deflecting the interested feelers she'd sent his way. He'd been flattered, of course, but he'd also been committed to his budding relationship with Sunny. Kirk had never cheated on Linda, though he'd had opportunities, and he wasn't about to turn into that kind of lowlife just because his ring finger was now bare.

The morning after his breakup with Sunny, he'd run into Allison in the library. In the course of their conversation she'd revealed that she was planning a gallery-hopping jaunt to SoHo that weekend and hinted that she wouldn't mind company.

Kirk had been on the verge of declining when the

rational part of him asked, *Why not?* He had to move on with his life. With any luck, a friendly outing with another woman would help him get over Sunny.

And he could certainly do worse than Allison Hyde, an accomplished, scholarly woman who was easy on the eyes. An ambitious woman who'd made something of herself. Exactly the sort of woman he could admire and respect.

Allison stared transfixed at the painting in front of her. "He conveys so much with just a few simple brushstrokes," she said, with all the authority of the art expert she was.

"Uh-huh," he murmured, for the umpteenth time since he'd parked his car just off Broome Street. That had been about a dozen galleries ago, which was eight or nine more than he would have preferred.

"What do you think of his use of color?" she asked.

The picture in question was a large canvas painted by a well-known contemporary German artist named Alvin Kraft—well known to people like Allison, anyway. Kirk had never heard of him before, but his work was currently featured at this gallery. The subject was a female nude, rendered in shades of red and black in Kraft's signature volatile style.

"I think this is one angry German," Kirk said.

Allison raised one dark eyebrow. "Interesting. What makes you say that?"

Kirk bristled internally. She probably didn't know how professorial she sounded. He was sure it was unintentional—this was a date, after all, not a class field trip—but after several hours, it was getting old. And he was also tired of politely deferring to her opinion and pretending to like crappy art.

"It's just like all his other work." He gestured toward the paintings surrounding them. "The same brusque style, the same discordant colors."

"Discordant?"

"You know what I mean. Look around you. This guy hates women."

Allison's eyes bulged. "Alvin Kraft is a very well respected artist! He had a show at the Guggenheim—"

"Allison, he can have a show at Buckingham Palace for all I care, it doesn't change the twisted way his mind works." Kirk steered her toward a painted papier-mâché statue—yet another female nude, Kraft's subject of choice. The headless form had a coarse ugliness that could only be deliberate. The exaggerated breasts and genitals were further accentuated with slashes of maroon paint.

Kirk said, "You're seriously trying to tell me this isn't the work of a grade-A misogynist?"

Her smug smile grated on his nerves. "Yours is a predictable response, based on a limited understanding of modern art."

Kirk laughed. He couldn't help himself. "I understand enough. I have eyes." Allison had just dropped several points in his estimation. How he detested that condescending if-you-don't-like-it-you-don't-understand-it nonsense.

"What I mean is," she said, "if you had a broader knowledge of the philosophy behind—"

"Allison, open your eyes!" Forcibly he planted her in front of the disturbing statue. "If my son ever makes something like this in art class, I'll hustle him off to therapy before the paint is dry."

With a resigned sigh she said, "All right, point taken. Kraft can be...abrasive." She turned to him excitedly. "But he got a reaction out of you, didn't he? He made you *feel* something. You're certainly not apathetic about him."

"Hey, I wasn't apathetic about the Hillside Strangler, either."

Allison recoiled at the comparison and shot a furtive glance around, clearly hoping no one had overheard his boorish comment.

Kirk was antsy, and not just because of the interminable gallery hopping. He wished his mother hadn't ordered him not to call and check up on Ian. She'd been adamant. He understood why. He did tend to overdo it—the result of sudden single parenthood, he assumed. In trying to be both father and mother to the boy, he always felt he was leaving something undone.

"Just have a good time," Mom had told him. "You have the beeper." Kirk had given her yet another lesson in how to call the pager, though she'd paged him before with no problem. He'd spent the day waiting for the thing to vibrate, only it never had. Which meant everything had to be fine at home. They were probably getting ready for dinner. He wondered if his dad had caught a bluefish. His mother couldn't stand bluefish.

The thought of food made his stomach growl.

"Listen," he said, "all I've eaten today is an apple I grabbed on my way out the door this morning. Maybe that's why I'm so cranky."

"Oh, poor baby. I had no idea you were hungry."

"Well, aren't you? I mean, we've been walking around SoHo for—" he checked his watch "—five and a half hours."

"When I'm looking at art, I forget about everything else. The truth is, I never eat much. I have a yogurt around noon between classes, and I usually stop at this soup-and-salad place for takeout on my way home from campus. I could go another five hours, no problem."

Kirk pictured Sunny and her healthy appetite—nourished by her love of cooking. Watching her eat was one of life's great joys.

With effort, he suppressed the wayward thought. He'd promised himself he wouldn't think about Sunny during this date with Allison, wouldn't compare the two women. Valiantly he tried not to wish it were Sunny marveling with him at this artist's blatant misogyny, as he knew she would, and laughing with him at the gullibility of the elitist art community that gobbled it up with a sterling silver spoon.

He guided Allison out of the gallery. "There's a steak place nearby," he said, watching her face as he said the word *steak,* and seeing the reaction he'd expected. Too bad. They'd done what she'd wanted to all day; now he was in the mood for a slab of blood-rare cow the size of Rhode Island. "You can get a salad there," he assured her as they dodged traffic and headed west.

"BY THEN ROBERT HAD BEEN sleeping on the sofa for nearly a year, so it wasn't really cheating." Allison speared an artichoke heart and washed it down with a swig of chardonnay. "I mean, we were separated, we just weren't *separated,* if you know what I mean, until the divorce was final. It's enormously expensive maintaining two households, so of course, we put it off till the very last moment."

Kirk found himself back in "uh-huh" mode as he carved a chunk off the best porterhouse ever to pass his lips. He smiled, recalling Sunny's words that day in early July when they'd shared a picnic lunch at the university. *Just tell me you didn't turn vegetarian on me.* She'd love this place; he had to bring her here.

Stop it! he commanded himself.

"Of course, the girls didn't really understand," Allison added, "but kids are resilient, they bounce back from these things. Don't you know, their dad now has this *wonderful, enormous* apartment on the upper West Side." She threw her arms wide as bitterness infected her voice. "Jennifer and Danielle each have their own room when they stay there. *Professionally decorated*, naturally."

"Uh-huh."

"And Daddy's live-in girlfriend is *so nice*. And so close to them in age—just like a *big sister!*" Allison tipped back her wineglass and drained it. "So guess who gets to be the heavy when the girls come home with assorted body parts pierced after a weekend visit with Daddy and his twenty-year-old trollop?" She gestured to the waiter for more wine.

The scientist in Kirk did some quick calculations based on alcohol consumed with respect to body mass—in Allison's case, a hell of a lot of the first factor and not nearly enough of the second.

He slid the bread basket toward her. "That little salad can't possibly fill you up. Why don't you order some grilled chicken or something?"

"I don't have a big appetite, remember?" she said.

Not for food, he thought, watching her hoist the refilled wineglass to her lips.

A conspiratorial twinkle lit Allison's eyes. "You must know Jane Birmingham. She's in your department."

"Yes, of course. Why?"

Harpooning a lettuce leaf on her fork, Allison leaned forward with a smirk. "*Well*, you know that welcome reception Wilton threw at his house the first week of class?" she asked, naming the university's president.

"Yeah..." Kirk had an uneasy notion where this

was leading, and he didn't like it. "Allison, I'm really not interested in my colleagues' private—"

"You know Wilton's wife was out of town, right? And no one can remember seeing Jane leave his place that night after the party."

"Look, this isn't—"

"So everyone figures she was the last one left. Simon Arby—he's in biochem, you must know him—Simon told me that Hank Kline's wife saw Jane and Wilton exchange a look that can only be called *heated*." She hissed out a sizzling noise.

"Allison—"

"But the clincher is..." Her knowing nod announced the coup de grâce. "The next morning? Jane's wearing the *same outfit* she had on the night before! A black pantsuit. You'd think she could've come up with something a little more appropriate for Wilton's reception." She snorted in amusement. "But hey, if *he* didn't mind...!"

Jane Birmingham was a fine physicist who had struggled for decades to overcome the sexism endemic in the world of scientific academia. Now here was one of her colleagues—a female colleague at that—trashing her name for sport. Kirk sighed. "Jane wears black pants and jackets most days. She has a whole collection of them."

Allison blinked. "How do you know that?"

"We're in the same department, remember?"

"Huh. She must think black flatters her figure.

Good luck with *those* hips." She took a deep swallow of wine.

"I'll be honest with you." Kirk set down his fork. "I have no stomach for workplace gossip."

"Gossip! I'm relating *fact!*"

"I've seen promising careers damaged beyond repair by unsubstantiated rumor. I have a policy. I don't spread it. I don't listen to it."

"Well, *excuuuse* me. I just thought you'd be interested in learning how Madame Birmingham got promoted to the head of *your* department right after that reception. Everyone *else* knows about it."

"Everyone else also knows that the previous department head, Bill Dunne, had to retire suddenly for health reasons. Jane has a long and distinguished career. She was the most qualified candidate, and the logical choice to replace him. If she *was* the last to leave Wilton's house, perhaps it was so they could discuss her new position."

"Oh yeah, I'm sure that was it," Allison sneered. "Couldn't be some *other* kind of position they were discussing. No, of course not." She stood. "I'm going to find the ladies' room."

Kirk watched her negotiate the trek to the john with a self-conscious attention to balance. He pushed away his plate and signaled the waiter for the check.

13

"YOU MISSED ALL the excitement," Kirk's mother said when he walked in the door. She was sitting in his living room, pulling clean clothes out of a plastic laundry basket and folding them into neat piles on the sofa cushion next to her. The TV was on—some raucous sitcom. She muted the sound with the remote control device.

"Mom, how many times have I told you, you don't have to do our laundry. I'm a big boy. I know how to sort the whites from the colors."

"Well, the hampers were full—it looked like it hadn't been done in days. I don't mind. It keeps my hands busy."

Chuckling, he shook his head. There was no sense arguing with Mom about some things. He plopped down on an easy chair. He'd tried to make it home before Ian's bedtime. Finding his mother parked in front of the tube, engaged in busywork, told him his son must already be in bed.

Kirk's father strolled in from the kitchen and settled himself on the other end of the sofa. "You missed some good fried bluefish, son. There's plenty left if you want some."

Kirk's mother grimaced in distaste. "Don't you dare bring those leftovers home, Fred."

"No, thanks," Kirk said. "I ate. What excitement did I miss?"

Mom folded a tiny blue T-shirt with a line drawing of Albert Einstein's face on it. Kirk had found it in a museum gift shop and hadn't been able to resist. "Ian had to go to the doctor," she said.

"What?" Kirk sat up. "Is he sick?"

"No, no, it was his arm." She added the shirt to the stack destined for Ian's room. "He's just fine now, so don't go getting yourself worked up. What was it the doctor called it? Tennis elbow? No, that wasn't it."

"Nursery something," Dad said, throwing an arm over the sofa back.

"Nursemaid's elbow!" Mom said. "That was it!"

"Nursemaid's elbow?" Kirk frowned. "I've never heard of it."

"It was dislocated," Dad said. "The doc, he took care of it. Pushed it right back in. Good as new."

"What?" Kirk was on his feet, headed for Ian's room. "When did you put him to bed? Is he asleep?"

"I don't know," Mom said. "Sunny's putting him in."

That was enough to halt Kirk in his tracks. "Sunny? What's she doing here?"

Dad scowled. "Why didn't you tell us you two called it quits?"

Kirk raked his fingers through his hair. "I don't know, it just..."

"Never come up?" Mom gave him her signature don't-try-to-pull-one-over-on-me look.

He sighed. Why hadn't he told his folks about the breakup? He opted now for honesty, for both his parents' sake and his own. "I guess I was kind of hoping it'd blow over and we'd get back together."

Mom's features softened in sympathy. "She still has feelings for you. I can tell."

"I know she does. It's...complicated. Did she, uh, tell you why we split up?"

"No," Dad said, "and we didn't ask. That's between you two. It's a shame, that's all I can say. I liked that girl way back when and I still like her. She's good for you."

Mom's clothes-folding motions became more abrupt. "Well, you know I agree with your dad, but it's not our business, really. It has to be your decision."

Kirk's mouth twisted. "It's Sunny's decision at this point." He glanced down the hall toward Ian's room. "But you didn't answer me. Why is she here?"

Mom said, "I called her when I couldn't get in touch with you. I thought you were with her."

His stomach turned into a lead weight. "You told her I had a date?"

"I thought you were with *Sunny!*" she repeated. "How was I to know..." She *tsked* as she slapped a folded washcloth on the pile destined for the linen closet.

"It's not your fault," he said wearily.

"I was so upset," Mom said. "Ian was in pain and he wanted his daddy, and I couldn't reach you, and Fred was out on the boat. I didn't know what to do. Sunny just dropped what she was doing and came right over. Took care of everything, bless her heart. I tell you, that girl is calm and levelheaded in a crisis. More than your old mama, that's for sure," she added with a self-deprecating smile.

This was a side of Sunny Kirk had never seen. But he wasn't surprised. During the past two months he'd begun to realize there were depths to Sunny Bleecker he'd never imagined.

Allison Hyde, for all her worldliness and advanced degrees, couldn't hold a candle to his Sunny.

"So." Dad must have been reading his mind. "Who'd you go out with?"

"Oh, another teacher from Garrison. Art history."

"That's an unusual name," his mother noted with a smirk, clearly picking up on his lack of enthusiasm.

"Her name's not important. I'm not going to go out with her again."

When he'd dropped off Allison at her house, she'd clung to him as if their tiff over gossip had never occurred. She'd invited him in for a drink and to view her art collection, including her most recent acquisition, a series of etchings by the latest darling of the art world—male and female nudes she described as "whimsically erotic."

Tell me this woman isn't asking me in to see her dirty

etchings, he'd thought, peeling her off him and mumbling some lame excuse.

Kirk turned to his mother. "What do you mean, you couldn't get in touch with me? I had the pager turned on all day."

"I called it and called it." When he started to respond, she snapped, "And yes, I did it right. But you never called back!"

"Too busy with the art teacher?" Dad snickered.

Kirk unclipped the pager from his belt and looked at it. The tiny LCD screen was blank. It should have shown the time of day. He stabbed the buttons, with no change. "Great. The battery died. Perfect timing. I *knew* I should have called to check up on him!"

"Now, don't start that," Mom said. "Don't you think I felt just awful that I told you not to call? Especially since it was my fault Ian got hurt."

"Now, don't *you* start!" her husband said. "The doc said it wasn't your fault."

"What did he say?" Kirk asked. "The doctor."

Mom said, "You'll have to ask Sunny for the specifics. She's the one who took Ian to him."

Kirk stared. "Sunny did that?"

Dad spoke up. "That girl really cares for Ian. It's plain to see."

"I know," Kirk said. "I know she does."

"Well." Mom folded the last item—a pair of Ian's baggy little neon-colored swim trunks—and set the stacks of clean clothes back in the baskets. "Now that you're home, we'll be on our way."

After seeing his parents off, Kirk made his way down the hall to Ian's room, and stood silently by the partially opened doorway. The room was dimly lit by the night-light. He could just make out Sunny bending over Ian's crib, stroking his back as she crooned softly to him. Kirk smiled, recognizing the familiar lilting melody of "Scarborough Fair," the only lullaby his son wanted to hear nowadays.

Her voice grew progressively quieter. After a while she stopped singing, but continued to stroke him, never taking her eyes off him. Finally she straightened, gradually lifting her hand from his back so as not to wake him. Silently she pulled the side of the crib up. Sunny stood staring at Ian for another minute, just watching him sleep. She pressed her fingers to her lips and touched his blond head, and turned toward the door with the most serene smile Kirk had ever seen.

She started when he pushed the door wider. He raised a finger to his mouth, and briefly touched her shoulder, passing her on the way to the crib.

If Ian had suffered some great trauma that day, Kirk could find no sign of it now. He slept peacefully, his little back rising and falling in the slow, regular pattern of sleep. "Good night, champ," he whispered.

Sunny was waiting for him when he quietly pulled the door shut behind him. "Thank you," he said, looking her in the eye, letting her see his sincerity and his gratitude and those deeper, richer feelings he wished he were free to express.

They stood that way for long moments, their gazes locked in silent communion. Finally she broke eye contact, with obvious effort. As the two of them returned to the living room, she said, "There's no need to thank me. I didn't do anything. It was Dr. Davidson who fixed Ian's elbow."

"But you got him there. You took care of him as if—" He didn't say the rest. He knew she heard it anyway. *As if he were your own child.*

He could be, he wanted to say. *You have a family here, Sunny—not your dream family, perhaps, but certainly mine.*

"Where are Fred and Marianne?" she asked, looking around the deserted living room. "Did they leave already?"

He nodded. "Mom told me to thank you again, for being—how did she put it?—so calm and level-headed in a crisis."

"She would've done fine without me."

"What exactly happened?" he asked.

Sunny filled him in on everything, from Marianne's phone call to the doctor's treatment and his advice for preventing a recurrence of the injury. She glanced around the living room. "Where'd I leave my purse?"

"Don't go," he said. "At least, have a cup of coffee with me first. A glass of wine. There's no need to rush off."

"I've had a long day." A funny look came into her eyes, before she redirected her gaze to the framed picture over his mantel, the central star-patterned segment of a quilt his great-grandmother had made decades ago. "And so have you."

There it was. The dreaded subject. The Date. "Stay just a few minutes. Let's talk."

"I really have to—"

"What's waiting for you at home that's so important?" he asked. "Do you have to wash your hair? Press your waitress uniform?"

She sent him a sharp look. Did she think his words were some sort of gibe about her job?

"I didn't mean it that way," he said. "You should know me well enough by now."

"Should I?"

"You know I respect you, Sunny—everything about you."

She stared at him a moment longer, then her features softened into a wry smile. "That uniform is pure polyester. Never been touched by an iron. I just..."

"You just don't want to talk to me," he finished for her. Before she could respond, he said, "I had a miserable time today." He flopped down on the couch, shoving the laundry basket away with his foot. "She was another teacher, and I thought it would do me good to go out with someone else."

Sunny's smile held no humor. She sat on the easy chair he'd occupied earlier. "So this was some kind of therapy, this date. Is that it? Like choking down bad-tasting medicine?"

Though he knew her words were mocking, Kirk chose to take them seriously. "Yes. I shouldn't have gone. It wasn't my idea—she asked me."

"Is she pretty?"

"Yes."

Sunny's gaze sharpened at his prompt response. Perhaps she'd expected him to equivocate.

"She's attractive," he said, "on the surface. I'd assumed there was something else going on behind the pretty face, something worthy that would hold my interest, but I was wrong."

"You didn't like her?"

"She lacks character," he said simply.

Sunny digested this a moment. "Why did you assume she was more than a pretty face? At first."

He took a deep breath and let it out. "Her career, her education level, God, even the way she dresses and wears her hair. I admit it, I jumped to conclusions."

Sunny wrapped her arms around herself. She didn't look at him. "It didn't take long for you to get better acquainted, though."

Something in her tone of voice...

Kirk sat up straight. "Sunny, what do you think happened between me and Allison today?"

"Allison? Nice name."

"We walked around SoHo," he said. "The galleries. For five and half hours. That's it. Oh, and we went to dinner, but I couldn't stomach her company for another minute, so we never got around to dessert. And no, I didn't kiss her."

Allison had kissed him, though, when he dropped her off—a sloppy, poorly aimed smack that landed on the corner of his mouth. Sunny didn't need to know that.

"I thought..." she said, "when Marianne said you weren't responding to your beeper..."

"What, you thought I was preoccupied? As in doing the wild thing with Allison? On our first date? Our only date," he hurriedly amended.

She shrugged. "It could happen."

"The battery in my pager went dead. Mainly what I was doing today," he said, "was thinking about you. And trying not to." He watched her carefully as he added, "After all, it's not like you and I have any real hope of a future together."

She said nothing. Kirk's pulse accelerated. Was she having second thoughts? He knew better than to press her, yet he couldn't hold back the words that spilled out. "Watching you with Ian just now...you can't hide how much he means to you, Sunny. It's right out there for anyone to see."

"I—I never denied my feelings for Ian."

Just your feelings for me, he thought. But that wasn't strictly true, either. She'd admitted that she loved him—or at least that she had before everything had fallen apart.

"Come here," he said, placing his hand on the sofa

cushion next to him. She shook her head. He rose and went over to her. In one agile movement he pulled her off the chair and sat in it himself, resettling her on his lap. She tried to rise, but his arms banded around her. She gave up the struggle, sighing in exasperation.

"I know you're confused," he said. "You want me to think you have it all figured out, that it's a black-and-white issue and your mind's made up. You'd probably like to believe it yourself. But that's not the way it is."

"Are you a mind reader now?"

She felt so good in his arms, and smelled better, that voluptuous citrusy scent that wafted from her warm, silken skin. "I don't have to read your mind," he said. "I see it in your eyes, the doubt, the feelings for me that you wish would go away."

On cue, she averted her gaze.

"You try to make this whole messy situation fit into these strict parameters you've set up in your mind," he continued, "but it's not so easy, is it, when your feelings won't cooperate?"

"I don't know what you're talking about. Define 'parameters,' Professor."

He pinched her bottom through her white jeans, hard enough to elicit an outraged yelp. "Don't give me that dumb little waitress act—you know exactly what I'm talking about," he said with a devilish grin. "You 'professor' me again and I'll spank you."

"You're trying to tell me I'm denying my true feelings, hiding behind these artificial barriers I've set up," she said. "Like my desire for a traditional nuclear family—including children of my own. Like my insistence that the man I share my life with not keep really really important secrets from me. Such as a *vasectomy!*"

"I've apologized for that," he said. "I wish I could say I'll never in my life do anything wrong or hurtful or just plain dumb again. I'll sure as hell try. I don't suppose you've ever done anything you're sorry for?"

She ignored that. "You make it sound like I'm so rigid. Like I'm fooling myself. I'm not fooling myself. I've always known what I wanted."

"It's good to know what you want." Kirk tried to pull her close to his chest; she stiffened. "It's good to be focused. But not to an obsessive degree. Then you're just a slave to some unattainable goal." She started to speak. He clamped his hand over her mouth. "I don't want to hear again about how everyone in the world but you gets to have this Ozzie and Harriet home life. We both know it's not true."

She waited patiently until he uncovered her mouth. "One crucial little detail seems to have slipped your mind. *You're* the one who broke up with *me.*"

"And you're the one with the power to bring us back together again," he said. "*Really* back together. Not just going through the motions like we were those last couple of weeks."

"All I have to do is abandon my lifelong dream."

"All you have to do is listen to your heart." Kirk pressed his palm to her chest, to the smooth skin revealed by the V opening of her sleeveless, beige linen blouse. "Stop running from where it leads you."

She closed her eyes; he could clearly see the battle being waged within her.

"I know," he said, rubbing her back in circles, "I know how hard it is, how confusing. Don't give up on me, on us. That's all I ask."

Sunny's eyes opened. She looked so lost, so vulnerable. This time when Kirk pulled her close to his heart, she didn't resist. She leaned against his chest, her head nestled in the crook of his neck.

When she spoke, he had to strain to hear her. "I admit this whole thing isn't as...one-dimensional as I wish. It's harder than I thought it would be to...to just end it." She snuggled a little closer to Kirk, as if seeking a refuge from the hailstorm of emotions buffeting her.

He bent his head, nuzzled her soft hair. "I may not be able to make all your dreams come true, but one thing I can promise you."

She raised her glistening eyes to his.

"No one could love you more," he whispered.

She held his gaze, searchingly. He cupped her jaw and lifted her mouth to his. Her lips trembled under his, and it was a shock to his system how good she felt, how much he'd missed this.

Sunny didn't fight the kiss. It was as if he'd broken

past some internal barrier and she was his once more.

At least for the moment.

Sunny's mouth moved under his, and when his tongue touched hers, she eagerly deepened the kiss. They clung to each other; he pulled her legs firmly against him on the big chair, ran his hand up her thigh to her hip. The air left her lungs in a breathless sigh as she drew her mouth from his at last.

"I have missed you so," he murmured, pressing soft kisses to her face. Her breasts brushed his chest with each breath, inviting his hand to stray higher.

Sunny's eyes fluttered shut, briefly, as he lightly caressed her through the beige linen. Automatically his fingers sought the sensitive peak, stiffening under her blouse and bra. Her breathing quickened; she leaned back a little, letting his other arm support her, to give him better access.

"I love the way you touch me," she murmured. "Your hands... You've always known just how to..." She ended on a breathy whimper.

Kirk soon became impatient with the fabric shielding her from him. She watched with slumberous eyes as he undid the tiny shell buttons running down the front of her blouse. Her bra came into view, cotton as always, with those luscious half cups, this time in blue checked gingham.

He ran a finger along the edge of the bra, following the slopes of her breasts. "You got a good tan this summer," he observed. "How far down does it go?"

She smiled impishly. "That would be telling."

"Then I'm forced to employ all the research skills at my disposal."

"The scientific method, huh, Professor?"

He mock-glowered at her. "Didn't I warn you what would happen if you 'professored' me again?"

Her smile grew mischievous. "You promised a spanking, as I recall."

He let his gaze rove up and down the length of her, perched on his lap. "You sound almost eager for me to flip you over my knee." Their sex play had never gone in that direction, but then, they'd only been together a couple of months before the breakup. As uninhibited as Sunny was, Kirk anticipated a lifetime of adventurous delights. If.

If they could find their way around this impasse. If they could manage to make their relationship work.

The kinky stuff would have to wait. All Kirk wanted at this moment was to share himself with the woman he loved and prove to her that she needed him as much as he needed her.

He pulled Sunny's blouse down her arms and tossed it on the nearby hassock. "I never saw this bra before. I like it."

"Thank you."

He toyed with the fly of her white jeans. "Do the panties match?"

He read the hesitation in her eyes. Without giving her a chance to stop him, he unzipped her pants and parted the fly to take a peek. Matching blue gingham, starting well south of her belly button. Sunny favored abbreviated bikini panties. The fact that they were cotton rather than some silky fabric was actually a turn-on for Kirk. He was a sucker for Sunny's brand of artless sensuality; she always managed to look sexy and innocent at the same time.

"This isn't a good idea," Sunny said as he swiftly stripped the jeans off her.

"This is the best idea I've had all day." The jeans joined her blouse on the hassock. Kirk laid his palm over the satiny skin of her belly, and felt her stomach muscles quiver. The bare upper slopes of her breasts rose and fell faster as he lightly stroked her stomach, paying extra attention to her navel, which he knew to be exquisitely sensitive. Holding her gaze, he slid his fingers downward, just over the top edge of her panties.

"Kirk..." She sounded out of breath, even a little panicky. "I—I haven't changed my mind. I mean, I still don't want to."

He could make her want to. He knew Sunny. He knew her hot buttons, her weaknesses. He knew where to touch her to make her shudder and moan and melt in his arms.

He could seduce her. He ached to do just that. But the last thing he wanted was for Sunny to regret making love with him. He decided that when she gave herself to him again—if she ever did—she wouldn't doubt that it was the right thing to do. She'd want him as much as he wanted her.

Until then...

"I know that," he said, and leaned down to kiss her. "That doesn't mean I can't give you pleasure."

"Oh no, you don't." She let out a shaky laugh and grabbed his wrist. "That's the same thing, really."

"Is it?" His fingers moved lower still, tracing the shape of her. The thatch of pubic hair felt springy under the thin fabric covering her mound. "See, I don't agree with that. Not at all."

He continued to caress her, languidly, and eventually the fingers clamping his wrist grew slack and dropped away. Her legs parted slightly; she probably wasn't aware of it. Leisurely he explored her feminine cleft through her panties.

Sunny sucked in a sharp breath. Her hips moved restlessly. She was holding on to him now, as if clinging to an anchor.

"I love the way you look when I touch you," he murmured. Her color was high, her eyes half-closed. "You're so beautiful, Sunny. You have no idea how beautiful you are."

He saw her struggle to focus on his face, his eyes, saw her open her mouth to say something—to put a stop to what he was doing, most likely. Ruthlessly he intensified the caress, and her words died on a full-throated groan that made him even harder, if that was possible.

"Relax," he said. "Just let me make you feel good."

Kirk slipped his hand inside the top edge of

Sunny's panties. He found her drenched with her passion, slick and hot and ready for him.

Suddenly he was tempted to take what her body offered, to seek the release he so desperately craved. She wouldn't blame him, he knew; she'd enjoy it as much as he. But it would bring them no closer to a true reconciliation, might even push them further apart. Exercising restraint had never been harder, even when he'd been a horny teenage virgin impatiently waiting for Sunny to give him the green light.

She squirmed in his lap as he stroked her saturated entrance, teased the stiff little nub. Her gasps fed his own hunger, clawing at him from the inside.

Glancing down, he saw his own deeply suntanned hand, looking big and dark and rough against the delicate blue-and-white fabric that half concealed it. The triangle of auburn curls was visible, her panties having been pushed halfway down her hips, now rocking in time to his rhythmic caress.

His gaze returned to her flushed face as he slowly pushed his finger into her. Her mouth parted on a ragged sigh. His hand moved in imitation of the act being denied that painfully tumescent part of him that leaped and twitched under Sunny's writhing bottom.

He said, "Open your bra."

She blinked. He saw the words register, saw her mull them over for a second before shaking her head.

"Do it," he commanded, never ceasing his probing caress. "Unhook it."

Sunny's fingers trembled as she obeyed. It was a front-clasp bra. The cups parted and he drank in the sight of her lovely full breasts, their rosy tips tightly erect and irresistible. He bent his head and sucked a nipple into his mouth, and felt her body's pumping response as her internal muscles contracted.

Kirk eased a second finger into her, as his thumb circled and stroked her clitoris. And all the while he fed on her delectable breasts, licking and suckling and lightly biting, letting her hoarse cries of pleasure guide his actions.

Sunny clung harder to Kirk; her nails dug into his arms. Her body strained and bowed as her climax rocketed through her. Kirk raised his head and watched it happen, watched her features contort as if she were in the throes of agony. He felt the gripping force of her orgasm as he continued to stoke it, heard it in the strangled gasps that escaped her. Nothing had ever sounded sweeter.

She collapsed in his arms, spent. He soothed her with whispered endearments, his gentle touch. Her eyelids fluttered open. He smiled with his eyes, releasing a pent-up breath only when he saw her answering smile. Leaning down, he kissed her mouth.

Sunny said, "I take it back, Professor."

"What do you take back?"

Smiling wider, she stretched like a supremely satisfied cat. "It *was* the best idea you had all day."

14

"I WISH I'D NEVER HEARD of the damn Wedding Ring. Cantaloupe or yogurt?"

Sunny stood with order pad and pencil in hand, while Amanda decided what to have for breakfast. It was always one or the other for the slender blonde, half a cantaloupe with low-fat cottage cheese, or a bowl of low-fat vanilla yogurt with granola and banana slices sprinkled on top. With jasmine tea. No caffeine for Ms. Coppersmith, thank you. Sunny wondered how much more opinionated her friend might get after chewing a mug or two of Waffle-mania's nerve-jangling java, and decided it was just as well Amanda was hooked on the flowery beverage. The diner kept jasmine tea in stock expressly for this one discriminating customer.

"Yogurt." Amanda lounged like a queen in the sun-splashed corner booth she preferred when dining alone. The various sections of the *Sunday New York Times* were spread out on the table in front of her; the business section lay on top.

Sunny had been a waitress long enough to know that most people hated to eat alone in a restaurant, and were conspicuously self-conscious when forced to do so. Not Amanda, who was sublimely comfortable with her own company, in whatever setting she found herself. Far from fearing that other diners were staring at her, she probably assumed they were, and why shouldn't they? It was as if she took for granted that she was the most attractive, interesting person in the room.

Sunny felt sorry for the occasional hapless, hopeful gentleman who approached Amanda to strike up a conversation. If her dismissive stare didn't scare him off, the deed could always be accomplished with a handful of well-chosen words that, though outwardly polite, were guaranteed to make the would-be Lothario slink away, mumbling apologies.

"You don't mean that about the Wedding Ring," Amanda said.

"The hell I don't."

"Well then, think about Raven and Charli. If it weren't for the Wedding Ring, they wouldn't have met Hunter and Grant."

And if it hadn't been for the Wedding Ring, Sunny thought, she herself wouldn't be trying to go about her usual day-to-day activities with this yawning emptiness inside.

Sunny was even more confused after last night. She should never have remained at Kirk's house after his parents left—there was a reason she'd avoided being alone with him. That reason became painfully clear when the afterglow wore off and she found herself nearly naked in the arms of the man she'd sworn to cut out of her life forever.

The man she loved.

She couldn't get his words out of her head. *No one could love you more.* She wished she didn't believe him. She wished she could cast him out of her mind and heart and look for someone else to fill that yawning emptiness.

The fact was, last night's sensual interlude had only served to further erode her determination to do just that. How was she supposed to stick to her guns when, hours later, she could still feel the heated imprint of his hands on her body?

"Sit down." Amanda nodded toward the bench seat opposite her.

Automatically Sunny glanced around for Mike, her boss.

"I just saw him go into the men's room with his crossword magazine." Amanda lifted her tea mug to her mouth. "He's good for twenty minutes at least. And the place is quiet for the moment. Sit."

Sunny sat. After patronizing Wafflemania for her entire life, Amanda knew its owner and his habits almost as well as his employees did.

"How's the archaeology dig going?" Amanda asked.

"It's grimy and exhausting and I absolutely love it. And I've also started to audit a class on the history of Long Island."

"Those two kind of dovetail, don't they? Local history and the excavation of a Native American village?"

Sunny nodded. "I've always been fascinated by that stuff. And to be able to do this hands-on work... I only wish I'd acted on it years ago."

"Well, you're doing it now. Look forward, not back." Amanda was silent for several moments, fiddling with her spoon. "You know, you were wrong."

Sunny frowned. "Wrong about what?"

"When you said that whatever I wanted, I'd gotten."

Amanda had to be referring to that conversation in the backyard of Charli's parents' house, Sunny remembered, when Amanda had painted Mrs. Rossi's fingernails.

"You know what I meant," Sunny said.

"I know what you meant, and you were wrong."

"But look at you." Sunny gestured toward her friend, elegantly turned out even on a Sunday in crisp twill slacks and a silk designer polo shirt. "You're beautiful, smart, you have a career anyone would envy. You own a popular, profitable children's magazine, for heaven's sake!"

Amanda turned bleak eyes on Sunny. In a quiet voice she said, "My second divorce... There was a time there I thought I just wouldn't make it. It was like I was stuck in this bottomless pit...."

"I know," Sunny murmured.

"No, you don't know." Amanda sat straighter; she pasted a thin smile on her face. "You knew what I would let you see. Most of it I kept..." She didn't finish.

Sunny swallowed hard. She'd known her friend had been in pain, and she'd guessed that pain went deeper than she'd admitted at the time. But Amanda had blustered her way through it as she did with everything else. Sunny and Raven and Charli had been supportive of Amanda; they'd been there for her. Perhaps they should have tried even harder.

Amanda seemed to sense the direction of her thoughts. "You guys did everything you could for me. It was me. I wouldn't let anyone see how depressed I was. I was afraid that if I let myself unwind too much, I'd just, well, I'd fly apart." She shrugged. "Anyway, I got through it."

Sunny reached across the table and placed her hand on Amanda's. "Why are you telling me this now?"

"I told you before, you have no idea how lucky you are. If either of my ex-husbands had loved me half as much as Kirk obviously loves you..." Amanda smiled sadly; her eyes were moist. "I would have given up a lot for that kind of devotion. It's rare and it's special and that's all I'm going to say about it." She pulled back. Her chin trembled just slightly, as if her control hung on a thread.

Amanda didn't usually open herself up like this, Sunny knew, even to her beloved Wedding Ring pals. The fact that she had chosen to do so now touched Sunny deeply.

Sunny said, "I just wish this whole thing weren't so..."

"Complicated?"

She nodded.

"Welcome to adulthood. Land of tough choices."

"Maybe that's my problem," Sunny grumbled. "Maybe I'm just too immature to appreciate what I have."

Amanda's lopsided smile told Sunny she heard the important part: that Sunny did, on some level, appreciate what she had. "No one can accuse you of being immature," Amanda said. "Pigheaded, obstreperous and downright clueless at times, but never immature."

"Well, thank you," Sunny said dryly. "I feel much better now."

Amanda's gaze lit on something behind Sunny. "Break time's over. You've got customers."

Sunny glanced behind her. And smiled. "My Sunday morning regulars. The MacLeods." Rising, she squeezed Amanda's hand again; she looked her in the eye. "Thanks."

Amanda winked at her. "Remember, yogurt, not cantaloupe."

"Gotcha."

Sunny grabbed menus and the coffee carafe and made her way to the booth where Jim, Emily and little Davey MacLeod were getting settled. Emily set something on the bench seat next to her. It took Sunny a moment to realize she was looking at an infant carrier, the kind that doubles as a seat. And bundled in the carrier was...

A baby! An Asian infant who appeared to be three months old at most.

"Who's decided to tag along today?" Sunny handed vinyl-bound menus to Davey and his parents, and poured coffee. Were the MacLeods babysitting?

Davey, seated on the opposite bench next to his father, bounced on his knees. "She's my new sister and her name is Jennifer and she doesn't eat real food or use the potty, she just drinks out of a bottle and poops in a diaper!"

"Your new sister?" Sunny shifted her quizzical gaze from Davey's excited face to his parents' broad smiles. "Oh. Is she adopted?" Sunny immediately felt foolish for asking. What other explanation could there be?

"That's right." Jim beamed at Jennifer, now sucking a pacifier and blinking at her surroundings. "We waited a long time for this little treasure."

"But not nearly as long as we had to wait for Davey," Emily added.

Sunny mentally tripped over that statement. Emily had to mean it had taken her a long time to get pregnant with Davey. These were the *MacLeods*, for heaven's sake! The picture-perfect, Norman Rockwell family that had been making Sunny jealous since Davey himself had been a newborn. Adoption was all well and good, but a family like this was the

genuine article. You didn't get this kind of together-
ness through—

"Jennifer's adopted just like me," Davey boasted,
"but she only came from Korea. *I* came all the way
from *New Jersey!*"

Jim and Emily laughed, and Jim ruffled the boy's
hair. "This guy is the best big brother. Tell Sunny
what you did this morning."

"I gave Jennifer her bottle!"

"You did?" Sunny's tone of voice told him how
impressed she was by his maturity. "Did she drink it
all?"

"Yep. And Mommy put a towel on my shoulder
and she put Jennifer on my shoulder and I patted her
back and she spit up and some of it got on my shirt.
Yech!" He slapped his forehead, hamming it up for
his audience. "It was *disgusting!*"

"All right, let's hold it down a little," Emily said,
chuckling. "People are trying to eat. They don't want
to hear about spit-up."

Jennifer started to fuss. Her mother reached for
her. On impulse Sunny said, "May I?"

"Of course. I think she just wants to get a better
look around," Emily said as Sunny set down the coffee carafe and carefully lifted Jennifer out of the carrier. "This is the most inquisitive baby," Emily continued. "Always needs to know what's going on.
Always needs to be in the thick of things."

"Davey was just like that," Jim said with a proud
smile.

"Is that right?" Sunny asked the baby, as she cradled the solid weight of her in her arms. "Are you a Curious George? Curious Georgina?"

"Curious Georgina!" Davey cried, delighted.

Jennifer stared fixedly at Sunny, her dark eyes alert and, yes, inquisitive. This tiny new person reminded her so much of Ian; not in physical appearance, certainly, but in the irrepressible exuberance with which she took in everything around her.

"She's beautiful," Sunny breathed, more to herself than to the MacLeods. Reverently she stroked the downy black hair on the baby's crown.

Something dislodged inside Sunny then, settling into its proper place like a well-oiled gear. A tightness she hadn't been aware of before this moment suddenly eased, leaving her wondering how she could have lived with it all this time.

And she knew what she had to do.

Jennifer's mouth opened in a huge yawn, displaying pink gums north and south. Sunny bit back a watery chuckle, shocked to find her vision swimming. She blinked back the film of tears and handed the infant to her mother.

"You're a natural," Emily said, her eyes too knowing.

Sunny dragged in an unsteady breath. "So I've been told."

"I want a waffle!" Davey hollered. "With blueberry syrup and sausages and grapefruit juice!"

Jim's mouth quirked. "What a shock." His son was nothing if not consistent.

Sunny felt more buoyant than she had in years. "Coming right up."

15

SUNNY SLIPPED into the lecture hall through its rear entrance and moved to the middle of the back wall. It was nine-thirty on Monday morning and she was already dressed for work, though she didn't have to be at Wafflemania until noon.

About two hundred students packed the hall. Kirk stood at the front of the room, his back to his Physics 101 class as he wrote on the chalkboard. "Force, in newtons," he said, scrawling an f on the board, followed by an equal sign and an m, "equals mass, in kilograms—"

This is so boring, Sunny thought, watching the students diligently scribble in their notebooks. *How do they all stand it?*

"—times acceleration, in meters per second squared." Kirk added an a next to the m, and turned to face the class. His ice-blue gaze immediately homed in on Sunny, leaning against the back wall. Surprise flashed across his face, causing most of his students to turn and see what had distracted him.

Sunny gave everyone a cheery smile and a little wave.

"Um..." Kirk glanced at the board, as if to remind

himself of what he was supposed to be teaching. "For example—yes?" A student in the front row had shot his hand up and now asked an incomprehensible question—incomprehensible to Sunny, at least, who began to fan herself with her hand. After a few cooler days and refreshing mid-September breezes, summer had reasserted itself this morning, with the mercury hovering around the eighty-degree mark. The lecture hall was uncomfortably warm and stuffy.

Kirk droned on in scientific gibberish, answering the student's question, his gaze occasionally flicking to Sunny in the back. They really should install air conditioning in here, she thought, reaching up to unfasten the top button on her waitress uniform. Watching her, Kirk stumbled over his words, managing to reestablish his train of thought only with a conspicuous effort.

"Yes. So. For example," he continued, "if a five-newton force is applied to a three-kilogram object in a friction-free environment—"

Sunny popped another button free.

"—the object, uh..."

The students waited. A few followed his line of sight to where Sunny stood in the rear, now in maximum cleavage mode, fanning herself and taking deep, deep breaths.

"The object, uh... If a five, uh, newton force is applied to a three-kilogram object in a, um, friction-free environment, the object will accelerate..." He paused, his gaze locked on Sunny, now executing a full body stretch, her back arched, her torso twisting this way and that. One of his students took his silence as a cue to complete the statement.

"Five-thirds meters per second squared."

Kirk blinked at the student. "What?"

"Five-thirds meters per second squared!" The kid raised his hands as if to say, *Right?*

"Yes," Kirk managed to answer. "Correct. Um...I think we'll knock off a little early today."

A grateful murmur arose from the students, who lost no time shoving books, pens and handouts into their backpacks and heading for the exits, as Kirk rattled off a homework assignment. A doughy young man with greasy hair winked at Sunny and thanked her as he passed.

Finally the last student filed out and Sunny had Kirk to herself. He slipped his notes into his battered leather briefcase and made his way to the back of the room. He stood in front of Sunny for several moments, his expression inscrutable. Finally he said, "I had no idea you were so interested in physics."

"Didn't I tell you I intended to audit some classes?"

"Well, if you ever decide to pull another stunt like this one, just warn me ahead of time so I can wear a blindfold." He set the briefcase at his feet and refastened her buttons. Slowly. Sunny wondered if he could feel her thunderous heartbeat under the hot-pink polyester. She closed her hands over his and looked into his eyes.

"I don't deserve you," she said, "but if you still want me..."

The intensity of his gaze threatened to burn her. He squeezed her hands, almost painfully.

Sunny swallowed hard around the lump in her throat. "If you still want me, then I need you to know...I can't imagine living my life without you. I'd rather have you and no children than a dozen kids with any other man. Please, Kirk. Take me back. I'm so sorry."

She choked out the last words through a sob, but Kirk was already folding her in his arms, crushing her to his broad chest.

"Don't be sorry," he whispered into her hair. "You have nothing to be sorry about. I love you, Sunny—God, I love you so much."

He kissed her, and kissed her some more, and when they finally came up for air, Sunny was grateful for the physics professor's strong arms grounding her to the earth, the laws of gravity having been miraculously suspended just for her. Or so it seemed, as exhilaration and relief and unadulterated love lifted her toward the stratosphere.

A voice nearby mumbled, "Uh...sorry..." They both turned to see a scarlet-faced youth snatching a textbook off the floor. "I left my, uh... Sorry." Head down, he bolted through the doorway.

Kirk called after him, "Have that late homework in my office by three, Mr. Farber!"

Sunny smacked him, laughing. "Leave the poor kid alone. He's been traumatized enough."

Kirk wrapped his arms around her waist and pulled her to him. "Do you mean it? About us?"

"I mean it."

"I know how important it is to you, Sunny, having child—"

She silenced him with a finger to his lips. "We already have a child. I couldn't ask for a more wonderful, precious son—even if it took me too long to realize how incredibly fortunate I am."

Kirk stroked her back. "There's always that reversal surgery."

"And there are other ways, too. I'm...well, I guess I'm more open to the options than I was. But the important thing is that we have each other. I need you, Kirk. As long as we're together, everything else will work out."

The truth of that warmed her from the inside out, as if she'd trekked too long through the cold, lonely night and finally come home to the glowing hearth that had been waiting for her all along.

She pulled his head down to kiss him, and this kiss quickly spiraled out of control, leaving them winded, clinging to each other.

Kirk's smoky gaze lingered on the buttons he'd so recently refastened. "We've gotta find someplace private."

SUNNY WATCHED KIRK close the door to his office and turn the lock. She watched him cross to the lone window and close the cream-colored vertical blinds. He'd declined to turn on the overhead fluorescent fixture, which was fine with Sunny. Sunlight filtered through the blinds, bathing the room and the two of them in a soft, inviting light.

He turned to her. "Take off your clothes."

Sunny laughed. "Don't be shy, now. I know how difficult it is for you to say what's on your mind."

Kirk stalked to the well-worn institutional-style sofa. He started heaving piles of books and file folders off of it and flinging them onto the floor. "It's been eighteen days since we made love, really made love—"

"But who's counting, right?"

"—and I'm more than willing to strip you myself, but if I try it, in my present enthusiastic frame of mind, I might just end up ripping that uniform to shreds. How will you explain that to your boss?"

She plucked at the ugly pink fabric. "Polyester, remember? Not so easy to tear."

He swept the last papers from the sofa and turned back to her, his expression more torrid than she'd ever seen it. "Try me."

The sweet burn that had begun when he'd refastened her buttons in the lecture hall now flared hotter, deeper. Sunny forced herself to think in practical terms. "Seriously. Won't somebody come knocking on your door? I mean, the classrooms are right out there. You told me yourself how accessible the faculty is at Garrison...."

As she spoke, Kirk started to unbutton his faded gray twill shirt.

She said, "What will, um, what will people think if you don't answer the door?"

He stripped off his shirt, revealing a broad, suntanned chest with a light covering of gilded hair. "They'll think I'm in here doing unspeakably erotic things to you." He loosened his belt buckle. "And they'll be right."

Sunny took a deep breath. "Someone must have seen us come in here together."

Kirk's smile was lopsided. "You're playing it mighty coy for a lady who, not ten minutes ago, practically did a striptease for a couple of hundred pimply freshmen."

She bit back a grin. "I'd waited long enough to get you alone. I couldn't wait a minute longer."

"Well, now you've got me alone." He dropped his jeans and kicked them away. His briefs followed. "So what are you going to do about it?"

Kirk stood before her utterly naked and thoroughly aroused—her ravening Viking, all banked power and sinewy lines and potent, golden, glorious virility. He took her breath away.

So. What *was* she going to do about it?

Sunny leaned back against Kirk's desk, wearing a silky smile that told him she was pondering the possibilities.

Slowly he approached her. "It's awfully warm in here."

"Mmm, yes, I've noticed." She picked up a yellow legal pad from the desk and started fanning herself with it.

He flicked the nameplate pinned to her uniform, just over her left breast. She felt her nipples tighten.

"You're way overdressed for this heat." He slid his hands under the hem of her dress. "What's this? I thought you hated panty hose."

"Silk stockings and garter belts don't exactly go with Reeboks," she said, indicating the comfortable white sneakers she always wore at work.

"But think of the tips you'd earn if you flashed a frilly garter now and then. You could make a buck every time you leaned over to refill someone's coffee cup."

"Gosh, I never considered the earnings potential of my underwear. What are you doing?"

Deftly unbuttoning her dress again, that was what he was doing.

"Can't have you expiring from the heat," he said.

Kirk undid three buttons and spread the fabric, revealing the top of her floral-patterned bra. From outside the window came the sounds of students calling to one another as they entered and exited the building three floors below. Muted conversation drifted to Sunny's ears from nearby offices and classrooms. Her worries about privacy resurfaced, only to evaporate as Kirk placed a lingering kiss on the heated skin he'd just exposed.

Sunny's breasts tingled. Suddenly her clothes did indeed feel too hot, too confining.

"I have just what you need," Kirk murmured. "Stay right here."

He crossed to the corner and extracted something from the small, cubelike refrigerator that sat on the floor. He returned to her, peeling white paper off the object, which she identified as a frozen juice pop. Orange.

"Just one?" she asked. "What about you?"

Kirk gave her a mysterious little smile. "We'll share." He sucked the end of the pop into his mouth for a moment, then lightly touched it to the hollow under her throat.

Sunny flinched at the icy contact. She let out a shaky little laugh as he slowly, methodically, dragged it down, and down some more, letting it drip into her cleavage. Then he lowered his head and licked the trail of melted juice, paying particular attention to the shadowed valley between her breasts.

"You see? I'm real good at sharing." He sucked on the pop once more, then placed it between her lips so she could do the same. The tangy orange flavor teased her tongue and excited her salivary glands.

"How about it?" Kirk asked. "You all cool and comfortable now?"

"Oh, no," she said. "Not by a long shot."

He licked a drop of juice off the frozen pop. "Then speak up. Where else might I be of assistance?"

Sunny unfastened more buttons, down her torso. She shrugged the top of the dress off her shoulders and let it pool at her waist. "I'm just so hot everywhere. It's driving me crazy."

"That sounds serious." Kirk stepped closer, crowding her with his naked body until she was forced to sit on the edge of his desk. She leaned back, bracing her palms on the desktop. He looked her up and down, taking in her inviting posture, obviously contemplating what part of her to "cool down" next. Kirk was generously endowed, and the sight of his erection springing high and proud between them made her light-headed with anticipation.

Kirk painted a trail of orange juice across her collarbone with the frozen pop, nudging her bra strap down her shoulder in the process. By the time he'd licked up every drop, Sunny was breathing fast. Kirk's knuckles felt rough and hot and erotic as he released the front clasp of her bra and pushed it down her arms.

He stared at her for long moments, and she felt the intensity of his gaze like the brush of a feather. Finally he stroked the juice bar down the side of her breast and around it. Sunny's back bowed; she sucked in a breath. He traced ever-smaller circles until raw sensation burst in her nipple as the frigid, wet pop touched it.

Sunny bit back a startled cry, all too aware of how

thin the walls were. She watched Kirk's head lower slowly, held her breath as his scalding mouth closed over the now frigid tip of her breast. She gasped, arching more fully against his voracious mouth. Patiently he devoured every last drop of the sticky orange juice. By the time he'd lavished the same loving attention on the other breast, Sunny was writhing on the desktop, tangling her fingers in his hair and pulling him hard against her.

"Here, hold this." He thrust the ice pop into her hand, pulled her off the desk and propelled her toward the sofa, stripping off her uniform on the way.

Sunny found herself lying on the lumpy sofa cushions, clad only in underpants, panty hose and her white Reeboks. She scooted over a little so Kirk could perch on the edge of the sofa near her hip. He stuck the pop in his mouth, grasped the waistband of her panty hose and pulled them down her hips. Then he held the frozen pop suspended inches above her navel. They both watched as a glistening drop materialized, hung quivering on the end of the pop and finally splashed into her belly button.

Sunny chuckled, feeling her stomach muscles jerk in response. Patiently Kirk let the juice melt—another drop, and another—until a little puddle filled her navel. Only then did he bend down to lap it up. Sunny had to have the most sensitive belly button in the world, a fact that hadn't escaped Kirk, who held her still while he sucked out every drop.

At last he straightened, thrust the pop into

Sunny's mouth and worked the hose and panties over her hips and down her legs. Within seconds her underwear and sneakers had joined the pile of clothes on the floor.

How bizarre, she thought, to be stark naked with Kirk in his office, of all places, while the life of the university carried on all around them. From a nearby classroom came a burst of laughter from what sounded like dozens of students.

Sunny tensed. She took the pop out of her mouth. "Is this a really stupid idea? Doing this here?"

"Are you kidding? It's my most brilliant research project yet. The thermodynamic properties of quiescently frozen confections. I should apply for a grant!"

"Oh, you'll be duly compensated for your efforts, never fear."

"So. Are you cool enough yet?" He commandeered the ice pop, now about half its original size.

Sunny cocked her head consideringly. "Well, to be honest, the more you try to cool me down, the hotter I seem to get. I'm just burning up. In certain places."

"You don't say. This intriguing effect will have to be thoroughly explored."

"Well, if you insist."

"I must."

"For the sake of science."

"Naturally." Kirk lowered the dripping pop and painted a line of juice from Sunny's hip down her thigh. She folded her arms behind her head, content to lie there and be the very willing subject of the professor's "experiment."

Kirk's hot mouth followed every icy stroke. Sunny bit her lips as he licked and kissed the juice from her thighs and the sensitive insides of her knees. In the process he raised one of her legs and propped her calf on the back of the sofa.

A shiver of sensual excitement raced through her. She was ready now, right now; she needed him as never before. But something—an indescribable gleam in his eye—told her he wasn't yet finished with his thermodynamic research. Her suspicions were confirmed when he held the juice pop poised just above the juncture of her thighs. Sunny held her breath as he slowly, deliberately, lowered it.

She gasped as it touched down between her legs, driving her hips off the sofa. Kirk pinned her to the cushions as he delicately stroked the cold, wet pop up and down and around her intimate flesh. Sunny was panting, laughing and whimpering all at the same time, fighting the strong arm holding her down, although she didn't want him to stop, not really. She'd never experienced anything like this startling sensation, fire and ice sliding wetly over the most sensitive, vulnerable part of her. He kept the frozen pop in motion, gliding, tapping, probing, so she never knew where she would next feel the slick and searing caress.

Sunny was only vaguely aware of Kirk tossing the remains of the pop in the wastebasket and lowering his head—until the blistering heat of his mouth right there wrenched an explosive scream from her.

She no longer cared if anyone else heard, and

clearly neither did Kirk, who was wholly absorbed in the moment as his fingers opened her for his rapacious mouth. Sunny clutched handfuls of his hair, her own shrill gasps ringing in her ears.

Swiftly he brought her to orgasm, with his lips and his tongue and his long, skilled, deliciously rough fingers. Sunny jerked half off the sofa, helplessly swept up by the all-consuming force of it.

The aftershocks still pulsed deep within her as Kirk lifted her up to sit on the very edge of the sofa. Kneeling between her legs, he grasped her hips and impaled her in one smooth, bottomless, brain-liquefying thrust.

Almost immediately, Sunny felt her body tighten once more, felt herself begin another heady ascent toward the pinnacle. She clung to Kirk's hard shoulders, wrapped her legs around his waist. He murmured to her as their bodies met and retreated, as he stroked the very depths of her—words of hunger and of love, of need and devotion and awe.

He braced a hand on the sofa back, tilting them both while supporting her with one sinewy arm, filling her deeper, riding her harder, spurring her toward yet another bone-jarring climax. She clung to him fiercely as it overtook her, shock waves of pleasure racing outward from the place where they were one. Kirk joined her then, stiffening against her with a deep-throated groan.

They remained like that for several minutes, locked together on the edge of the sofa, touching and kissing and reveling in the pure wonder of it. Finally they shifted to lie side by side, still entwined.

A knock sounded on the door, jolting Sunny out of a near doze. Kirk didn't react, just continued to stroke her back in lazy circles.

With a wry smile she mumbled, "Aren't you going to answer that?"

"Sure thing." He yawned; his eyes remained closed. "I'll just hop up and pull open the door. What the hell. I don't need this job."

Another knock, louder this time, as a youthful voice called, "Dr. Larsen?"

Someone else said, "He's not in there, Snider. Let's go get something to eat."

"Larsen's always in his office after class. I need an extension on those labs."

"Again? Come on. Maybe the dining hall's still got some of those bacon-and-egg bagel sandwiches left."

"Jeez, Cassell, you already wolfed down two stacks of pancakes and a ham steak—give that big gut of yours a rest." Snider knocked again, more insistently. "Dr. Larsen!"

Cassell barked, "He's not in there!"

"Anne-Marie Rasmussen saw him go in right after class," Snider insisted, "with that redhead from the back of the lecture hall."

"The hot babe in the pink outfit? You dweeb!" Cassell snickered, his voice low. "Larsen's in there, all right—he's prob'ly got her bent over his desk right now."

Kirk's eyes opened. He cast a speculative glance

over his shoulder at his cluttered desk. He asked Sunny, "When do you have to be at work?"

On the other side of the door, Snider said, "Are you kidding? Larsen eats, sleeps and breathes physics. The guy wouldn't know what to do with a fox like that. She's gotta be, like, his sister or something."

Kirk muttered, "Mr. Snider's cumulative average just dropped several points."

"I'm going to breakfast," Cassell said. "You coming or what?"

"Ahh, I'll catch him this afternoon." Snider's grumpy voice trailed off down the hall. "You ever think of getting your cholesterol checked, Cassell?"

Sunny idly played with Kirk's crisp chest hair. "Are you going to give Snider that extension?"

"Sure I am. Right after I figure out what to do with a fox like you."

"His hungry friend seemed to have an idea." Sunny snuggled closer to Kirk, finding him hard already. So much for eating, sleeping and breathing physics. She smiled. "And since you asked—I don't have to be at work till noon."

"You don't have to be at work, period." Kirk leaned up on an elbow. "You can quit now. Today. And don't tell me you love your job, because I know you don't. I can support us. It's only a professor's salary, but it's pretty secure and I get good benefits."

"Well, I have to go in today—I can't leave Mike in the lurch. I have to give him notice so he can find someone to replace me."

A wave of giddy anticipation suffused Sunny. She

could quit her job at Wafflemania! Never before had she let herself even consider it.

"We're really going to do it, aren't we?" she breathed, awestruck by the stunning knowledge that her lifelong dream was about to become reality.

That dream had evolved from the simplistic fantasies of a starry-eyed adolescent to the more profound and enduring desires of the seasoned woman she'd become. Thanks to the patient love and devotion of one incredible man.

"Never let it be said I didn't do the thing properly." Kirk sat up. He took Sunny's hand in his. His blue, blue eyes seemed to glow from within as he said, "You will make me the most ecstatically happy man in the world if you agree to marry me, Sunny. I can't perform miracles, but this I can and do promise. I will do everything in my power to make you happy in return."

"You already have." Sunny pulled him to her and kissed him, her head swimming with the joyous, intoxicating prospect of waking up next to this man for all the days yet to come. By the time they broke off the kiss, they were breathless and laughing, dizzy with the unadulterated perfection of it.

"Noon, you said?" Kirk checked his wristwatch and gave her an unrepentantly wicked grin. "Want to help me get that desk cleared off?"

_____Epilogue_____

DON'T YOU DARE CRY. Amanda called on every ounce of willpower to keep her emotions in check as the organist struck up the wedding march. She stood with the rest of the attendants in the vestibule of the Episcopal church that Sunny's family had attended for generations. The interior of the cozy post-and-beam structure was dominated by warm oak, and stained-glass windows splashed rainbow bursts of morning sunlight across the assembled guests. It was the ideal setting for Sunny and Kirk's wedding.

Kirk stood on the dais at the front of the church, looking tall and straight and extraordinarily handsome in a dark, double-breasted suit. He was accompanied by the priest and his cousin Ryan, who served as best man.

Amanda was a bridesmaid, along with Charli, Raven, Sunny's youngest sister, Samantha, and Kirk's older sister, Anne. Sunny's other sister, Jill, was her maid of honor.

In deciding what her bridesmaids should wear, Sunny had taken a cue from the last Wedding Ring bride. When Charli had finally gotten her big church wedding in July, she'd asked her three Wedding

Ring pals to be bridesmaids, as well as her many sisters and a passel of cousins. With so many varied tastes, colorings and body types, Charli had invited each woman to wear a pastel dress of her own choosing. The result had been dazzlingly eclectic, the long church aisle resembling a field of multihued wildflowers as the female attendants walked down it in pairs.

Being the freest spirit among the four best friends, and having suffered through her own share of ugly, froufrou-laden bridesmaid dresses, Sunny, too, refused to impose her taste on anyone else. Thus Amanda now wore a slim, tea-length column of silk illusion with a matching opaque underslip, in the pale ice-blue that flattered her fair coloring. Charli wore a fitted lilac-colored gown with cream accents, while Raven had chosen a long, flowing peach sheath. Samantha and Anne wore pale lemon-yellow and a muted apple-green, respectively. They all carried bouquets of white bouvardia, a pretty tubular flower.

Kirk's groomsmen were the first ones down the aisle, which was decorated with swags of iridescent tulle and fragrant, multicolored flowers. The bridesmaids followed, single file. As she passed row after row of beaming guests, her smile firmly affixed, Amanda felt her throat tighten with a jumble of emotions, her delight in her friend's newfound happiness tempered by thoughts of her own failed marriages.

But that won't happen to Sunny and Kirk, she thought. Sunny had waited so long to find the right man, only to discover that he'd been there all along in her heart and her bittersweet memories, her first and only love. Amanda didn't doubt that Sunny would make Kirk a wonderful wife. Just as she knew for certain that he was thoroughly devoted to his bride.

The attendants arranged themselves on either side of the dais as Jill Bleecker, the maid of honor, joined them, followed by little Ian, the ring bearer, looking heartbreakingly adorable in his miniature suit and bow tie. He'd been paired with Kirk's seven-year-old niece, Maggie, who, in her capacity as flower girl and self-appointed baby-sitter, kept the toddler focused on his task and steered in the right direction.

Finally the bride made her procession down the aisle. Like Raven before her, Sunny was accompanied by both her mother and her father. Amanda had helped Sunny choose her gown, a feminine ivory confection that looked spectacular on her. The fitted, strapless bodice was adorned with vertical tucks and a sprinkle of ivory and pink silk flowers across the bust. The full skirt was a floor-length froth of ivory chiffon, layer upon layer of the filmy stuff over a more substantial silk underskirt.

Sunny wore her wavy auburn hair loose, the sides pulled back by antique silver combs and adorned with the same varieties of fresh flowers that made up her neo-Victorian bouquet: forget-me-nots, lady's slipper orchids, eustoma, poppy pods and champagne roses.

Sunny kissed her parents and joined her groom on the dais, her expression a mixture of unquenchable joy and soul-deep serenity. Amanda felt her throat tighten in sheer happiness for the friend she loved as a sister.

Not one tear! she commanded herself. *Everyone knows you don't do tears, even tears of joy. You're the damn ice queen!*

Okay, maybe ice queen was overstating it. Amanda had never been accused of being cold-hearted or distant—at least not by anyone who really knew her. But neither did she put her feelings on display. Bitter experience had taught her to play it close to the vest.

The wedding service was both dignified and moving. Even Amanda could appreciate it, and she wasn't one for organized religion. When Sunny and Kirk recited the parts they had written themselves—celebrating their rediscovery of each other and the wonder of the bond they shared, both as a couple and as a family—Amanda found herself perilously close to losing it.

She bit the inside of her trembling lip. Her vision wavered; she scratched a nonexistent itch on the bridge of her nose, swiping at the damp corner of her eye.

Charli, standing next to her, whispered in her ear, "You're busted. I saw that."

Amanda barely managed to contain the gust of laughter her friend's words triggered.

"Want a tissue?" Charli asked.

"You have tissues with you? Where?" Charli's elegant, curve-hugging dress had no pockets that Amanda could detect. It was the kind of dress Charli would never have worn before she'd met Grant. Back then she'd considered herself too plain and frumpy for body-conscious clothing.

Charli patted her gown's attached cummerbund. "Under here," she whispered, her own eyes moist. "I just know I'll need them before this thing is over." With a sly grin she added, "And so will you."

Amanda's friends knew her too well. She might fool the rest of the world, but not these special women she'd known since kindergarten.

The wedding wrapped up with an enthusiastic newlywed kiss and the traditional pelting of rice at the church steps. The wedding party and the eighty guests reconvened at a beachside restaurant with a sun-drenched, panoramic view of the Atlantic Ocean through two walls of picture windows. Hors d'oeuvres and mimosas were followed by a delicious buffet brunch, while a string quartet provided delightful background music.

Sunny and Kirk made the rounds to all the tables, greeting each guest in turn. The parents of all the Wedding Ring pals were in attendance, as well as Grandma Rossi, the picture of ninety-something elegance in her best black dress and plum-colored fingernails, courtesy of Amanda, who had become her personal manicurist.

Amanda knew that Kirk had phoned his late wife Linda's parents in California to tell them about his remarriage and to personally invite them to the wedding. They'd accepted the news with grace and affection. This was what Linda would have wanted, her mother had told him, even as she'd wept at this final proof of her loss. Kirk had assured them that they would always be an important part of the family, that they were still his much-loved mother- and father-in-law, and that he'd make certain they saw Ian regularly. Linda's parents hadn't been able to make it to the wedding, but they'd invited Kirk, Sunny and Ian out to California for Thanksgiving.

The couple had decided to postpone their honeymoon until February, when Garrison University closed for winter break. They already had reservations at the best resort in Cancún.

After the meal and the cake and the many toasts, some poignant, some funny, all warmly sincere, the four Wedding Ring pals kicked off their shoes, grabbed their elegant jackets and wraps, and strolled outside onto the beach. Seagulls wheeled in the unbroken azure sky on this brisk, early October afternoon. The endless expanse of sand was deserted except for a handful of hardy beachgoers in sweaters and sneakers, or bare feet and rolled-up jeans, meandering at the water's edge, occasionally stooping to retrieve a seashell or a surf-tumbled stone. A couple jogged by in shorts and T-shirts. A teenage boy searched for buried treasure with a metal detector.

"So." Amanda pushed her wind-whipped hair out of her eyes as she turned to Sunny. "Are you used to it yet? Not having a job to go to?" Sunny had worked at Wafflemania until a little over a week ago, when her boss had found a replacement.

Sunny grinned, holding the layers of ivory chiffon up off the wet sand as she edged closer to the water. "You'd be surprised how quickly you can get used to not wiping down tables and asking 'Decaf or regular?'"

"Well, you're not exactly a lady of leisure," Raven said. "A toddler edging into the terrible twos can be a handful."

"A very welcome handful," Sunny said. "And as much as Marianne and Fred adore him, I get the feeling they're just as happy not having to baby-sit every day while Kirk's teaching. Their energy level isn't what it used to be."

Charli said, "Now they get to be the kind of grandparents who coo and cuddle for a little while until Junior starts acting up, at which point they can turn around and hand him right back to Mom or Dad."

Amanda saw a self-satisfied smile crease Sunny's face when she heard the word *Mom*. Sunny was a mom now, at long last—perhaps not biologically, but in every other way—and she couldn't be happier about it. Neither could her friends.

"What are your plans?" Raven asked Sunny. "I

know you must have some. As rewarding as it is to raise Ian, I can't picture you being content with that for long."

"You know, it's funny," Sunny said. "I'd always assumed I *would* be content with being a mother, but now I'm not so sure. It was certainly enough for my mom."

"Your mom had *four* kids on her hands," Amanda reminded her. "Big difference."

"Maybe you'll have a few more someday, too," Charli told Sunny.

"Well, we'll see." Sunny swiftly backed away from the water's edge as a wave surged ashore. "Kirk made an appointment to reverse his vasectomy. We're keeping our fingers crossed. But whether it works or not won't change anything between us. I'm blessed and I know it. And after running around after Ian for just a few days, I've got to wonder..." She rolled her eyes. "How on earth did my mom do it with four?"

"With any luck, you'll get a chance to find out," Raven said with a tender smile.

"So what *are* your plans?" Amanda asked, pulling her blue velvet wrap around herself and chafing the gooseflesh from her arms.

Sunny bit her lip. "I did something without telling you guys."

"Not allowed," Amanda said dryly. "Every detail of your life must be submitted to the Wedding Ring for review."

Raven asked, "Is that another of those mysterious rules that keep cropping up?"

Charli couldn't contain her curiosity. "So tell us! What did you do?"

Sunny's eyes sparkled. "I applied to Garrison as a regular student. I'm going for my B.A."

Amanda gasped. "Get out!"

Raven's eyes went wide. "Did they accept you?"

Sunny spread her chiffon skirts and executed a little curtsy. "I start in January."

Her friends squealed in unison, startling a nearby trio of seagulls dining on a crab carcass.

"It'll take me a while to earn my degree," Sunny said. "I'll be going to college part-time, so it won't interfere with raising Ian. He's my priority now."

"You little sneak!" Amanda cried. "How could you keep this news from us?"

"I didn't," Sunny said. "I just told you."

"Yeah, *now!*" Amanda said. "We could've been rooting for you. Sending positive vibes your way. We're your best friends! The *Club Nuziale.*" That was what Charli's grandma Rossi used to call the foursome even before they'd established the Wedding Ring, when the girls, typical teenagers, had been fixated on boys. *Club Nuziale* meant the "Wedding Club" in her native Italian.

"It's funny. Before I fell in love with Kirk...again," Sunny said with a lopsided smile, "I shared everything with you guys. Every detail of my life," she added, parroting Amanda's words. "The three of you were, well, you were my support system. Like my family. Closer than family in some ways. You still are, only…well, it's different now."

"I understand," Raven said, and glanced at the others. "I think we all do. It's not that you love us any less, it's just that you've found your life partner—your soul mate, whatever you want to call him. It's only natural that your relationship with everyone else is going to change, evolve—at least a little. I experienced that when I married Hunter."

"So did I," Charli said, "when Grant and I fell in love."

Amanda stood mute. She couldn't claim to have had similar feelings when she married her two ex-husbands—more evidence, perhaps, that she hadn't been a satisfactory wife, that she hadn't committed herself unreservedly to the one relationship that was supposed to supercede all others. She wanted to believe what her friends had assured her, that the fault had lain with Roger and with Ben, not her. But deep in her heart she knew that when it came to marriage, she was a failure. And always would be.

She might be able to convince herself otherwise if not for one inescapable fact: both her husbands had left her, not the other way around.

Raven, perceptive as always, seemed to sense her disquieting thoughts. "Does the birthday girl feel any older?"

"Not at all. Yesterday was a day just like any other."

Charli said, "I wish you'd let us throw you a party. The last of us to turn thirty—that needs to be celebrated."

"Sunny's wedding preparations took precedence," Amanda said. "I'm not some little kid who needs to get her birthday candles and pointy hat."

"Well, we'll have to make up for it with a belated party," Sunny said. "Birthday candles, pointy hats, hell, we'll even throw in a clown."

"Maybe a pony ride if you're really good," Raven added.

"We'll make it a surprise party if we have to," Charli warned her, "so no use fighting it."

Sunny rubbed her hands together. "And then the real work begins."

Charli shot her fist. "The last Wedding Ring bride!"

Amanda stiffened her spine. "You ladies must not have been paying attention, or perhaps you've gotten carried away by the romance of the day. I distinctly recall informing all of you—repeatedly—that I have no intention of walking down the aisle again. Ever."

"Nice try," Raven said. "You swore an oath, along with the rest of us—"

"When I was eighteen!" Amanda threw her hand out. "I did a lot of stupid things when I was eighteen!"

"The Wedding Ring isn't stupid," Charli said.

Amanda sighed. "I know it worked for you guys,

and that's really wonderful, but face it. I'm not in the same situation. None of you were married before. I was. And let me tell you, two failed marriages are more than enough wedded bliss for one lifetime."

Sunny said, "Humor us. Let us introduce you to one man. One! If it doesn't work out—"

"No." Amanda remained immovable. She knew that if she showed the slightest sign of weakness, she'd have no peace from her matchmaking buddies. "Any efforts on your part to set me up with a man will only result in embarrassment for all of us. I will not cooperate in any way, shape or form. I will not date the guy. I won't even talk to him. That's my final word on the subject."

Sunny, Raven and Charli exchanged looks, silently gauging one another's reactions.

"So that's it," Amanda said, sensing that her friends had reached an agreement, knowing what that agreement had to be. After all, they had no choice but to back down in the face of her obstinacy.

So where was the relief she was supposed to feel?

"All right, then," Amanda said. "It's settled, and I won't hear another word about any matchmaking. Agreed?"

Her friends exchanged another long look, this one punctuated by devilish grins.

"Wedding Ring husband-hunt number four." Sunny cackled. "This one's gonna be fun!"

Pamela Burford presents

The Wedding Ring

*Four high school friends and a pact—
every girl gets her ideal mate by thirty or be
prepared for matchmaking! The rules are
simple. Give your "chosen" man three
months...and see what happens!*

Love's Funny That Way
Temptation #812—on sale December 2000
It's no joke when Raven Muldoon falls in love with comedy
club owner Hunter—*brother* of her "intended."

I Do, But Here's the Catch
Temptation #816—on sale January 2001
Charli Ross is more than willing to give up her status as
last of a dying breed—the thirty-year-old virgin—to Grant.
But all *he* wants is marriage.

One Eager Bride To Go
Temptation #820—on sale February 2001
Sunny Bleecker is still waiting tables at Wafflemania when
Kirk comes home from California and wants to marry her.
It's as if all her dreams have finally come true—except...

Fiancé for Hire
Temptation #824—on sale March 2001
No way is Amanda Coppersmith going to let
The Wedding Ring rope her into marriage. But no matter
how clever she is, Nick is one step ahead of her...

*"Pamela Burford creates the
memorable characters readers love!"*
—The Literary Times

#1 *New York Times* bestselling author

NORA ROBERTS

brings you more of the loyal and loving,
tempestuous and tantalizing Stanislaski family.

Coming in February 2001

The Stanislaski Sisters

Natasha and Rachel

Though raised in the Old World traditions of their
family, fiery Natasha Stanislaski and cool, classy
Rachel Stanislaski are ready for a *new* world of love....

*And also available in February 2001 from
Silhouette Special Edition, the newest book in the
heartwarming Stanislaski saga*

CONSIDERING KATE

Natasha and Spencer Kimball's daughter Kate turns her
back on old dreams and returns to her hometown, where
she finds the *man* of her dreams.

Available at your favorite retail outlet.

Where love comes alive™

Visit Silhouette at www.eHarlequin.com   PSSTANSIS

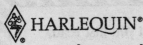

From bestselling
Harlequin American Romance author

CATHY GILLEN THACKER

comes

TEXAS VOWS

A McCABE FAMILY SAGA

Sam McCabe had vowed to always
do right by his five boys—but after
the loss of his wife, he needed the small-town security
of his hometown, Laramie, Texas, to live up to that
commitment. Except, coming home would bring him
back to a woman he'd sworn to stay away from.
It will be one vow that Sam can't keep....

On sale March 2001

Available at your favorite retail outlet.

HARLEQUIN®
Makes any time special ™

Visit us at www.eHarlequin.com

PHTV

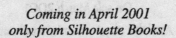